# RISE OF THE PHOENIX

## Guardians of the Phoenix

JL Madore

**JL Madore**

Cover Design: Gombar Cover Designs
Note: The moral right of the author has been asserted.
This is a work of fiction. Names, characters, places, and incidents either are the product of the author's imagination or are used fictitiously, and any resemblance to actual persons, living or dead, business establishments, events, or locales is entirely coincidental.



**Rise of the Phoenix: Guardians of the Phoenix**
**JL Madore** -- 1st ed.
ISBN: 978-1-989187-37-1

# CHAPTER ONE

*Calli*

*Flying*. The sensation of vaulting from a fast-moving vehicle as it collides with an immovable object strikes me as both terrifying and exhilarating. Time freezes as inertia smashes me through the windshield and hurtles me toward the graveled shoulder. My life races before my eyes, and it is a short, pathetic tale. California riffraff dies in a cross-state chase, while hunted by a pissed biker gang. The End.

Life sucks.

Death, too, apparently.

Wind rushes over me, the farm-fresh air tainted with the metallic tang of blood, the burning of oil, and the throaty rumble of a dozen Harley chopper engines.

I soar behind the surge of power brought on by Kia Rio meets power pole. Broad daylight. Straight road. Wrong time—wrong place. Mom and Dad would be so proud.

I always envisioned me and Riley turning things around and getting whisked away to become international spies or something. Maybe the reason we went through so much as teens was to prepare us for what was to come.

I crash to the asphalt with life-shattering force, flipping and breaking bones as I tumble across jagged stones and into the ditch. The impact jars every bit of life out of me.

So, this is it. The big D.

Dead at the side of some rural route in the middle of northern Texas nowherelandia. The crazy thing is. I'm not scared. Maybe I'm jaded, but life has been shitty, death can't be much worse. Without Riley, why bother anyway.

Whatever comes next—bring it.

*Jaxx*

TRAFFIC ACCIDENT – PEDESTRIAN STRUCK

POSSIBLE EXPOSURE – NYMPH ADOLESCENT

12 M ALERT. ABNORMAL BREATHING.

DRIVER - HUMAN

35 F UNCONSCIOUS.

PD NOTIFIED. FS NOTIFIED.

FCO ON ROUTE.

I read the dispatch description as it appears line-by-line on the responder screen on the dash of my truck. Twelve-year-old nymph hit by a car at eleven o'clock in the morning? "Come on, people. It's a school day for shit's sake."

In a perfect world, kids—human or fae—would be spared the violence of reality. They'd grow up laughing and acting like idiotic fools, and blending in with human society, not being mowed down by a car and bleeding in the streets. But six years of living among narys as a first responder to the Fae Concealment Office has taught me that this is far from a perfect world.

Exhaling an unsteady breath, I stare out the windshield and hold my course for home. I finished my block and have the next three days off. The only things on my horizon are the b's of bliss: breakfast-beer, bacon, and bed.

Glancing to the steering wheel controls of my truck, I hit volume up and blast Little Big Town singing *Boondocks.* With both windows open and my hand riding the current of a warm Texas breeze, I press the pedal and let the growl of the engine rev. Life is good.

A spot on the horizon up a ways catches my eye. I lean closer to the dash to squint past miles of cornfields. There's a rising line of smoke. A human gaze wouldn't register it, but my heightened preternatural vision picks it up without issue.

Not that I see much. A single, wispy line of darkness rises against an otherwise bright blue sky.

Thomas Rhett comes on the radio next and, yeah, I agree with the guy. I've seen his wife in the video. Blondes are my weakness, too. He can *Die a Happy Man.*

I'm belting it out, serenading the scarecrows, when I come upon that smoke signal rising to the heavens. The stench of burning oil and gas is thick in the air. I park beside the mangled Kia and drop out of my truck.

The wreck isn't much different than any other.

A punched-out windshield and no driver in the seat.

That's never a good sign. I follow the trajectory of

the ejection and yep, one roadkill warrior flung into the ditch. Shit. Why even have seatbelts in cars if nobody's gonna use them? Hustling over, I take a knee and reach under her hair to check for a pulse.

*Damn.* Fifteen minutes ago, that gravel and blood-tangled mess was likely a gorgeous mane of gold.

I lean close and take a long whiff of her scent. Human.

Her skin is still warm, but without a pumping pulse, it won't be for long. The unnatural angles of her arm, knee, and wrist suggest her body shattered in a dozen places. Yeah, that, and a chunk of her skull cracked open like a hard-boiled egg on the asphalt. D.O.A. Such a waste.

"I'm sorry, darlin'. Dying out here all alone is a damn shame."

With nothing to be done but call it into the local PD, I head back to the mangled Kia to see if I can find any ID. The car is a beater piece of shit, Frankensteined with a mismatched door and a primer-painted rear quarter panel. The back seat is an ode to takeout containers, but I find her purse wedged between where the pole stopped and what used to be the passenger seat.

No chance of getting the thing out in one piece. I grip the bag and give it a good haul. The strap snaps and I pull it free. Opening the passenger door to my truck, I set the purse down and fish around for a phone case or a wallet—

A rush of magic hits my back and tingles over my skin. As the hair on my neck stands on end, the scent of char fills my sinuses. I turn back to eye the scene. Is the car about to blow? That doesn't happen nearly as often for reals as it does on TV. Opening my gifts wide, I sense a steady build of magical tension. I lift my nose and test the scents on the breeze.

The air reeks of smoldering flesh...

It's coming off the woman.

Jogging back over, I take in the smoke steaming off the tattered rags that used to be her clothes. W.T.F.? I reach down to pull her up onto the gravel shoulder but hit a wall of searing heat. Staggering back I raise my hand to shield my face.

She is burning up. Like literally—*burning up.*

Human combustion isn't real, is it? As the magical tension in the air nears critical mass, it pushes out from the woman like a latex balloon filled past its limits, thinning as it nears detonation.

Potential energy pushes at the air around us. I back off fast and barely turn in time to save my face from the blast.

The woman's body goes up in a fiery ball of flames.

In six years living among humans, and all my life witnessing the fae world strange and unusual, I've never seen anything like it. That woman erupted into a raging fireball of human flame.

I gauge the height and brilliance of the inferno and cuss a blue streak. That will draw attention. As a sworn duty officer in the FCO, preventing exposure of the magically unexplainable is part of my job.

I'm torn. Spontaneous human combustion is bizarre but doesn't technically fall under the category of *other*.

The distant scream of sirens solidifies my resolve. Okay, human problem, human solution. How do I explain the woman catching fire? Maybe the car caught on fire, and she got caught up in the aftermath of the blast?

It's a stretch, but the fire chief is in my pride. He'll fudge the rest. Right. Stage the scene. I hop to it and grab the jerrycan out of the utility box in my truck bed. One flick of a handy-dandy lighter and *whoosh*, the car goes up in flames.

"Mmmph…"

The throaty female grumble makes me yip and jump clear of the ditch. Frickety-frack.

The dead woman moves. I check that no one heard me whimper like a schoolgirl. Nope. My reputation for unending masculinity is safe.

Flailing a weak hand, blondie brushes at her face and groans. Okay, that's just wrong. What the hell is she? And yeah, I guess we are solidly in *other* territory now.

I run over and lean in close. With my mouth open, I draw the air over the scent receptors in my tongue. Pulling her scent into the full depths of my lungs, I purr, long and low. She holds a heady mixture of feminine strength, char, and something that triggers my jaguar to prowl forward.

*Mine.*

I can't explain that reaction even if I wanted to. My body ignites as I scan her naked curves. The fire blast burned away her clothes, and she lays gloriously bare and unmarred by the accident. Shame. On. Me.

Mama taught me better, but I can't look away.

As a hot-blooded alpha male, my cock growing hard

could be an involuntary physical response. I've never gotten roadside randy over a crash victim before, but regardless, I can still excuse it. I'm more concerned with my jaguar's primal need. My wildling mojo is thrumming beyond all logic.

It strikes me then—the legends I learned as a cub.

No *waaaay*. That can't be what this is*, can it?*

Holy shit!

*Brant*

"Damn it, Brant, hold him still, or he's going to hurt himself."

"You're worried about *him?*" I adjust my boots in the shifting mud, struggling to guide Chocolate Mousse, a sixteen-hundred-pound bison, into the portable med-chute. "He might've been more agreeable if you hadn't castrated him the last time he was in this thing."

The furry ass fights to swing his massive head around to get a look at Doc's tools. I struggle to hold the line, cracking my knee against the wall of the chute. With a firm grip on the beastie's horns, I work the slow and steady to back him up.

"A few more steps, big man…" I grunt, throwing more shoulder into the effort and digging in for another push.

Mousse isn't known for his congenial disposition. In fact, in a pack of sixty-two, he is the biggest, most stubborn son-of-a-bastard we have, which is why we are in this situation. "You gotta learn to play it cool with the ladies, dude."

Mousse responds to that by stomping his hoof and

splattering a glop of rank-smelling muck up my jeans. “That better be mud, Mousse, or I’m barbequing your ass.”

Gritting my teeth, I dig the toes of my boots in and give it hard. My massive thighs burn with the effort, and my muscle-banded arms blow well past the rubbery ache of overdoing it. I’m a fucking enforcer for the FCO. On the daily, I fight twenty-foot trolls and swamp monsters and rogue warlocks. Why am I letting this oversized pot-roast get the better of me?

“Stop being such a stubborn ass,” I grunt.

Another stomp and another splat of filth flies. This one catches me in the face and my bear growls. Nope. Not mud. I fight not to gag. “That was low, Mousse. Stop being such a prick and get into the fucking chute.”

Head down, body thrumming, I stop playing nice and release my grizzly. My animal roars forward, rising to the surface with a surge of cocksure power to get the job done. The bison on the farm are afraid of our bears, but the time for being a nice guy ended when I started eating shit.

I growl, meeting the beast’s gaze with my own. My bear’s presence glows in my golden eyes, and the beast will not only see it but sense it.

Mousse snorts and backs up fast.

When the latch of the gate clicks behind me, I let off a roar. “Yeah, that’s right. Fuck you, Mousse.”

Doc laughs. “Get out of there before he tramples you.”

That’s all I need to hear. I climb the slatted sides of the metal chute and up-and-over it onto the pasture grass.

Lying flat on my back, I yank off my gloves and swipe the gritty manure out of my mouth. "That's nasty. Tell me again why I'm here doing this instead of out saving the world?"

"You didn't let the Wookie win, R2."

I cough as oxygen gets reacquainted with my heaving lungs. Oh yeah, I kicked the FCO squadron leader's ass the other night during the annual wargames. The military stuffed-shirt smiled through the loss like a gentleman, but the next day, I was cycled off rotation while upper management 'reviewed' personnel files.

"Those pencil dicks at FCO headquarters need to learn a big paycheck doesn't make them big men. Just because they have administrative clout, doesn't mean we grunts have to bow down on every front—or that we're too dumb to see what's going on."

"And what *is* going on?"

I don't want Doc involved in that mess… whatever it is. "I'm just saying that you practice like it's real or else you end up dead in the field. Where in the playbook does it say I had to let him win?"

"Nowhere. It's a common sense thing."

"Yeah, well common sense isn't my strongest suit."

"And that's exactly why you are home spitting bison shit instead of living the life you love." Doc stands over me, his short-cropped hair as dark as his bear's black pelt. "Enough rest. Get your lazy ass up and hold him steady so I can sew up this gash."

"Then we head inside for breakfast. I'm starving."

"Even after your manure amuse-bouche?"

"Har-har," I say, the bitter taste still pissing off my

grizzly. I draw a deep breath and shake off the muscle quakes. Back on my feet, I round the chute and reach through the slats to push the bull against the rails. "Work, work, work. All work and no play makes Doc a dull boy."

Doc looks up from stitching. "I'll survive."

"But will it be a life worth living?"

Doc pulls the suture hook and tightens the black loop of the stitch until the bison's pelt pinches together. Rinse and repeat. Each time the needle gathers more fur and flesh, another trickle of scarlet pulses from the cavity of the gaping wound down the round of Mousse's side.

"I'm serious, Doc. You're a catch: ex-military hero turned home-town doctor. The ladies eat that shit up."

Doc laughs. "You coming on to me, big boy?"

I roll my eyes. "You wish. What I've got going on is too much bear for you."

Doc continues his work. The guy is a damn talent with the doctoring. "You get enough play for our entire brood, my brother—when you're not covered in shit, that is. Today, not so much. You reek."

I shift my stance and secure my hold. Mousse is losing patience with this whole process. "I clean up good. And the ladies like a big strong male with the heart of a teddy bear."

"And modesty. That goes a long way too."

One minute, I'm laughing with Doc. The next, a weird buzzing lights off in my skull. My world shifts and I tilt my head, searching the sky for a plane, or a swarm of those crazy murder hornets I might be hearing.

Nothing.

I shake my head, but the sound doesn't clear.

Did I get knocked in the noggin?

"Yo, Brant. Pay attention."

I stare into the distant sky. The buzz expands from my ears into my cells. I reach toward the morning sun and feel a fiery heat ignite inside my chest. "I have to go."

Doc laughs. "Yeah, right. Breakfast will be there—"

I straighten and start back. "Sorry, Doc. Gotta go."

"Brant, what are you… Hey, we're almost done. What's wrong with you? *Brant!*"

*Nakotah*

My claws rip into the earth as I dodge the rough-barked trees and slick roots jutting up from the forest floor. The pithy ground offers me traction to dig in and propel myself forward on the hunt of the rabbit that has no chance against me. *Sorry, Bugs, it's lunchtime.*

As a man, I blend into the student body of my university and pretend that life on two feet is enough for me, but as a wolf, when I'm running the private lands of my father's forest corridor, only one truth exists—this forest is my home.

Mine to run in, to hunt, to play without fear of hunters, to drink from cold streams, and not worry about pollution. The energy of these twenty-two-hundred acres of protected land pulses in my veins as powerfully as the strength of my lineage in my royal wildling blood.

I overtake the rabbit in a brilliant lunge.

The panicked hare kicks in my jaws, twisting in a brief but brave attempt to break free. I flick my head and clamp my maw down with enough force to end the creature's suffering.

The coppery tang of warm blood seeps into my mouth, and I can't help the grumbling of my stomach. Animal instincts win out when I'm in wolf form. A rush of dry air breezes past and ruffles my thick coat.

A storm is brewing.

I lift my muzzle, breathing past the downy fur of the rabbit, wondering what has my hackles raised. Scents drift to me from near to far. The smell of the wood-chip path shifting under the tough pads of my paws comes first. Beyond that, other forest smells sift in: leaves, wet soil, distant animals.

Nothing out of the ordinary.

In the distance, a chipmunk shrieks as something startles it on the forest floor. What has me so on edge?

I push through the trees. Twigs lash at my muscled forequarters as I trot toward the village, a fresh kill hanging from my mouth. A shiver of anticipation races up my paws from the earth and quivers through my body. It is an indescribable blend of excitement, resolve, and fae magic.

A storm is brewing.

And it's calling me.

*Hawk*

"And a rogue group on the western coast is being investigated by human law enforcement. A large money exchange was traced back to a robbery of a gun depository. Preliminary reports from the intel team put the offenders squarely in our camp. How would you like to proceed?... Mr. Barron, sir?"

I pull my attention from the view of the cityscape out my forty-fourth-floor boardroom window, scan the expectant faces of my Fae Concealment executive team, and meet the inquisitive gaze of Jayne, my personal assistant, and self-appointed fiancée.

"Are you with us, darling?"

I smile at the eight men sitting around the table and close the sitrep folder on the table before me. "Thank you, gentlemen. We'll finish this another time. Proceed as you see fit."

Jayne stiffens as my executive team scrambles to take their leave. She knows better than to question me.

As the room clears, I move to the glass wall. What is this sensation burning inside me? After unbuttoning my cuffs, I roll my sleeves to just below my tattoos. Then, I loosen the Windsor knot of my tie. My wildling senses are firing, beckoning me to strip down and take to the air.

Why? What calls me?

"You're so tense," Jayne says, running her hands down the back of my tailored, Tom Ford shirt.

I adjust my stance to ease the pinch of my boxers beneath my slacks. Why am I so aroused? I close myself off to the fire growing center-mass in my chest. I am the master of my actions and won't be drawn in by animal instinct alone. Still, it's a fight. Nothing like this has taken hold of me before.

Jayne's gaze narrows in the reflection of the glass.

"Are you rethinking our engagement?"

I chuff. "How can I rethink something I gave no thought to in the first place?"

She rolls her eyes. "You're in a mood."

I won't marry Jayne. She likes to pretend that when she suggested it, and I didn't answer, it signaled consent.

No. The proposition simply warranted no response.

As a ferruginous hawk, the largest and most deadly species of hawk on the planet, I am a bird of prey, a predator who refuses to be caged.

Clipping my wings would kill me.

I give the horizon one last aching look and turn. The drape of fabric at the front of my slacks hides nothing, and Jayne notices immediately. Her body reacts on a primal level: the widening of her pupils, the slight intake of breath, the stroke of her tongue to gloss those full, painted lips.

She craves what I offer—as women do.

Power. Charisma. The promise of breathtakingly hot sex with no boundaries. She will deny it to the end of days, but the woman is submissive to her heated core.

That's how I like them—loyal, willing, and hungry to please. And, in my current state of primal demand, I need my PA to personally assist me with a cock as thick and hard as the marble Corinthian columns in the outer foyer.

I run a hand down her blouse and frown.

The closer I draw to her, the less interested I become. That is new. I am hard and hungry but know down to my razor-tipped talons that Jayne isn't the one to quench this sexual hunger. Interesting.

Not being one to spend time on a dead issue, I sidestep her, round the boardroom table, and stuff my laptop into my bag. Slinging my suit jacket over my arm, I cover the party in my pants and head for the door. "Call Lukas. Have him gas up the Navigator and bring it around to the lobby entrance."

"What? You're leaving? It's two in the afternoon. The Monster Rights Conference is in less than two weeks. What about the fae land contracts? And the internal innovations announcement?"

As founder and CEO of the biggest fae security corporation on the planet, there hasn't been a day in over a decade that I haven't worked until well after dark. Not today. I'll never get any work done with my body and mind at war as they are. Filled with an anticipation, I don't understand, I set my sights on figuring out what's affecting me.

My heart pounds with what I can only describe as an insatiable need, and I want to sate it. "Clear my calendar for the week. It seems I have a personal matter to attend to."

# CHAPTER TWO

*Calli*

I wake nauseous, with a muddy heaviness in my head and silky softness against my cheek. The two sensations don't mix. How many mornings have I stirred to consciousness, wondering where I was and what happened the night before? I open my eyes, and the brilliance of morning light spears into my skull, forcing me to close them tight again and regroup.

Wetting my dry lips, I fall back on my black-out-Betty party days. Living on my own since fifteen, I indulged in poor decision making and bad behavior enough that waking up like this isn't an all-together foreign event.

Well behaved women rarely make history, right?

Like Riley always says… *said*. Past tense.

*A happy childhood makes for a boring adult.*

I rub the ache in my chest. Boring isn't a word that could ever be used to describe my BFF. Riley lived life on fire and was snuffed out way too soon.

As the fog hanging over my brain starts to burn off, I focus on the here and now—which is—where and when?

I draw a deep breath and a memory flickers through my mind. I was driving NASCAR fast… Sonny and the Sovereign Sons caught up to me. *Riiiight*, the power pole.

The echo of bones cracking and crunching in my head brings me fully back to the present. I lift my hands, amazed I can move. Not only move, but without any residual pain. The shift of my legs under the heavy wool blanket makes me startlingly aware that I am naked.

I bolt upright. My head throbs with a blood-rush, and I squint at the fancy bedroom. I'm lying on a mahogany sleigh bed with a swath of golden light casting its warmth through a French-door walkout. The décor of the room is elegant, with gold damask flowers covering the walls, brocade curtains, and a floor-to-ceiling beveled mirror in a heavy gilded frame. The reflective surface faces the glass doors and the illusion it creates, expands the space beyond its actual huge dimensions.

Swanky. *Waaay* nicer than any place I've ever slept—or stepped foot in—legally at least. I rub a hand over my face and stare out the French doors to a backyard that looks like a botanical garden. None of this rings any bells.

Well… other than alarm bells.

"How did I end up here?" Not on my own steam. I remember that much. "And why am I naked?"

I grip the edge of the blanket and look down at myself. An overwhelming rush of heat whooshes through my body as I take stock. It doesn't look or feel like anyone did anything vile while I took a stroll through unconsciousness.

That eliminates Sonny and the Sons having me. But knowing them, they wouldn't pass up a chance to make a buck. Those assholes have their dirty dicks in everything, guns, drugs, illegal gambling, human trafficking… *Shit.*

Did they sell me to some twisted, moneybags perv?

Where the hell are my clothes?

The last thing I remember is crashing out of my car and dying. Okay, so maybe I'm dead. That makes as much sense as anything else.

Muscles tense, I gather the blanket around my shoulders and hop off the bed. Testing my balance for a second or two, I confirm I'm steady and then head toward the dresser. A swatch of familiar green canvas makes my heart flutter.

My purse.

I give it a quick inventory. Everything seems to be here: wallet, twenty-seven dollars, phone, condoms, and the little scrap of paper tucked in my tampon carrier with a Texas address scratched down on it.

*Booyah!* The first piece of the puzzle slips back into place. "Take from me and I'll take from you, assholes."

Drawn into the dark recesses of my mind, I revisit the battered image of Riley's body when I found her in that alley. No way will other women suffer at the hands of these monsters. Not while breath still fills my lungs.

I can't wait to see the look on Sonny's face when I sucker-punch him in the sac and he realizes he's lost everything… and that I'm the one who toppled his world.

With Riley's fate fresh in my head, I shake off my car crash ordeal and try not to look at things too closely. Somehow, I am up and about. She died. I lived. Sonny and his goons will pay for taking the only thing I had in life.

The clothes lain out for me still have sales tags on them. Okay, so likely not dead. If this is the afterlife, I doubt LuLu Lemon makes yoga pants for the Pearly Gates Mall.

Or maybe they do. That *would* be heavenly.

Tossing the wool blanket, I finger through the outfit and by-pass the underpants, because, *ew*, I'm not wearing undies some stranger bought for me. That's creepy.

I do, however, pull on the pants and a cotton t-shirt.

Whoever purchased these has an eye for a woman's size because they fit perfectly, though I despise pastels.

I am more endless night than sweet delight.

After a quick trip to the loo, I tie the snapped ends of my purse strap into a knot, sling it over my head, and stuff the address of Razor's family property back into my tampon carrier.

Light glints off the back of a silver brush and comb set laid out on the dresser and I consider the value of what they might be worth. I scoop them up, toss them into my purse, and zip things up.

Smart or stupid, choices matter. With no idea where I am or who has me, I may need to barter or trade for a favor.

Raised male voices in the rooms below have me padding toward the closed door. My fairy clothes-mother didn't leave me any footwear, so barefoot is my new reality.

The volume of the argument downstairs bolsters and muffled shouts overlap. Maybe they're arguing over who gets the first go at me. I'm not interested in what's being said, but I am thankful for the heated commotion.

All the better to mask me taking my leave.

I half expect the French doors to be locked, but no. This little bird is free to fly the coup. Padding across the stone terrace, I peer over the iron rail and gauge the two-story drop to the lush grass below. No problem. I've snuck in and out of enough windows that this is cake.

A knock at the bedroom door behind me brings my hesitation to an end. "Calliope? I hear you're awake. My name is Jaxx. May I come in?"

I grip the rail, kick my feet over, and vault into the air. Warm wind rushes past me as my cells burst to life. A good jump always triggers a surge of exhilaration. It's a rush. As I near the impact of the manicured lawn, I relax, roll, and rise to my feet in what is without a doubt the most graceful move I've ever managed.

*Hubba-wha?* Where did that come from?

The perfectly trimmed grass feels like plush velvet on the bottoms of my feet. I push off and pick the closest point of cover. A man yells behind me, but adrenaline kicks in, and I'm not stopping to ask directions.

"Calliope!" he calls. "Hold up."

For one split-second, I wonder how he knows my name. Then, I remember the ID in my purse. I don't look back. If this was a standard roadside rescue, I would've woken up in a hospital, not naked in a mansion.

Something is *waaay* wrong.

I blow past the rose garden and round a gazebo. The sound of distant traffic spurs my hope. If I make it to the road and flag someone down, I'll—

A massive wolf cuts in front of me and halts my escape. It races past in a silver and chocolate blur, then prowls back around to stand in my way. Head down, shoulders rigid, it stares at me through dark, brown eyes.

Every hair on my body prickles upright.

*Holy-crapamoly*. I freeze and hold out my hand. Yeah, like that'll keep the beast from killing me. Where the hell did he come from? Heart hammering, I ease a slow step backward and scan to my right.

A grizzly bear lumbers close, its massive form only twenty feet away. It shakes its boxy head, thick brown fur ruffling beneath his broad shoulders. His big, black nose twitches as he sniffs the air and grunts, looking annoyed.

Heat builds in my chest.

Left then. My head swivels to my other side to assess my chance of escape. A golden jaguar sits silent as death, pegging me with an eerie turquoise stare. His head drops low, its shoulders tense and strung with coiled muscle.

What is happening?

My gaze flips left and right, a pounding in my temples making everything fuzzy. I know better than to turn my back on predatorial animals, but I am surrounded. When the flap of powerful wings sounds directly behind me, I spin toward the house I just escaped from.

A massive bird lets off a piercing screech and drops from the sky. As its talons stretch toward the grass, its form shifts, and a man touches down in its place.

What. The. *Hell?*

As the birdman straightens, I catch a glorious glimpse of tattoos and his manliness before clothes appear, and he is covered in slick black slacks, and a blue button-down rolled to his elbows. He's handsome without an ounce of pretty, and ruggedly masculine. "Calliope," he says, his voice hard and sharp. "Stop and let us explain."

The dominance of his voice resonates inside me. His tone is commanding and arrogant. It demands submission and I struggle to fight it and stay focused.

I look around. The bear flashes into a beautiful brunette beast of a man in cargo pants and a muscle shirt. He is beyond buff, with well-built shoulders and a brawny chest that fills out his towering frame. "There's no need to run, beautiful."

The wolf straightens and transforms into a young man with the rich copper skin and ebony hair of an indigenous American. He is shorter than the other three but wiry and fit. Wearing a denim shirt, ripped jeans, glasses, and a wide leather choker around his throat, he takes my breath away. "No one here will harm you. In fact, it's quite the opposite."

That only leaves—I turn to the jaguar.

The blond hottie that materializes before me is sexy beyond my wildest: tanned, golden skin, with bright turquoise eyes, and a glorious ruggedness that Chris Hemsworth would envy. Packaged in tight black jeans and a supple, linen shirt that hangs open at the front and swaths to his hip, I have a glorious view of the prettiest sculptured abs I've ever seen.

*Damn.* Riley would *squee* if she saw him—well, them.

I'm struck stupid. I've cozied up to a few perfect specimens during my wild and rebellious adventures, but these four put them all to shame. Four stunningly gorgeous men.

*And they're mine.*

I blink, wondering where *that* bizarre wave of possession came from? Before I sort out the cyclone of heated emotions swirling inside me, the hottie blond guy raises his palms and smiles. "Calliope, I'm Jaxx. I get that you're confused, but if you come on back to the house, we'll get things sorted."

*Sorted?* I've been kidnapped by Magic Mike and his troop of sexy shifter strippers. How do you sort that out? *Play it cool.* I can't escape four of them. I have to play nice until I see my chance to escape.

"Calli," I say, checking that the others aren't moving in while I'm distracted. A breeze comes up and I rake my fingers through my hair and out of my face. "I go by Calli. Who are you? Why am I here?"

"Wouldn't you be more comfortable inside?" asks the young native guy. He has a gentle voice and a striking kindness in his warm, brown eyes. I find him utterly disarming and raise my guard. Yeah, no. Less than three minutes ago, he had four legs and fangs.

"No. Out here is fine."

Jaxx nods. "Three days ago, I found you in a ditch on the side of the road. Do you remember being in a wreck?"

I drop my chin, my muscles tensed to run if an opening presents itself. These guys seem to sense my intentions because they remain hyper-focused and coiled to spring.

"Great," Jaxx says, his Texas drawl as sexy as his smile. "So, when I found you, the impact of the accident had done a number on you. I checked your pulse, and you were VSA—vital signs absent. You were dead."

Yeah, I sorta remember that.

"Then, to my mind-blowin' surprise, your body burst into a fiery ball of flame, and you resurrected. When the fire died down, the breaks in your bones had healed up, and the blood and trauma from the accident were gone. You were reborn."

I snort a laugh and wonder how they're keeping straight faces. Are they new? Am I supposed to believe this?

"Your skin was still hot as Hades in July," Jaxx continues. "I wrapped you in a fire blanket and got you out of there. I figured this was a better place for you, since the exposure of the unnatural is the last thing we need, considering..."

I read his expectant gaze, but I've got nothing. "Considering what?"

Jaxx frowns. "Considering you're a phoenix."

Okeydokey, time to go. My chest is so tight I can barely breathe. A breeze picks up and the sweet scent of honeysuckle drifts around me. It carries with it the unmistakable smell of an expensive cologne, irritation, concern, and manly musk. Whoa, my mind stumbles on that. How can I pick all that out of a breath of fresh air? I must have hit my head. "I'm just a girl who drove too fast and poled her car."

"And died," Jaxx adds. He gives me a tight smile, which I might believe is sympathetic if not for him being a jaguar-man holding me hostage.

"Uh-huh. And you guys are what, my welcoming committee to a kinky five-way in the afterlife? I don't think so."

His brow tightens. "That's not what this is about."

I read the guilty faces staring at me and a shiver of sexual awareness tingles over my skin. Their wanton gazes are subtle, but their seductive urges sing to my core. My heart races. My mouth waters. As tempting as no-strings sexual carousing with four sexy strangers seems, life doesn't work like that.

"Sorry, not buying it. Your come-hither vibes are off the chart, and I assure you I won't be making any reservations for a party of five in my sheets."

The bear chuckles and the bass rumble hits me right between my legs. He's brawny and beautiful, and his flop of shoulder-length brown curls does all kinds of things to me.

"We're wildlings, Calli," he says. His voice is a deep, rich rumble that tightens my nipples. "Whether shifting form is in your bloodline or this is a magical development from of out of nowhere, you are now one of us. And, if you're honest, it's not only us feeling the attraction. We smell your interest, and it's a heady scent."

*Okaaay*, time to leave. The fact that I am in a dire

situation, and my girl-bits are weighing in at all, is wrong. There must be a way to get clear of these guys.

I need to figure it out.

"Obviously, you're all very pretty but you can't be that bright if you think I'll fall at your feet. How did you do that animal shifting trick? Did you drug me?"

The native kid who transformed from the chocolate and silver-colored wolf looks confused. Gawd, his hair is chestnut silk and flows down nearly to his waist. The way the breeze picks it up, I can imagine how soft it is. I want to run my fingers through it, and have it drag across my naked flesh.

Heat builds in my core and a pulsing beat pushes between my legs. I close my eyes to fend it off. Why am I so horny when my life is in danger? I look them over, and my wanton grows wild within me.

The four of them groan. Jaxx and the bear adjust their footing, the hawk curses, and the native kid blushes. How can they share my discomfort?

"Calli," the young wolf says, "we each felt the pull of your magic the moment you resurrected. Jaxx was with you here in Texas, but Hawk, Brant, and I were as far away as we could be in the continental United States. Without any contact with each other, we knew to come. Something about who and what you've become called to us."

"Uh-huh." I eye him up and down. He doesn't look crazy but talking magic and resurrection doesn't scream sanity. And the hot thrum of my sex drive doesn't bode well for them. An aphrodisiac? Yeah, I bet that's what this is.

They roofied me—the bastards.

That explains at least part of it. Before now, I've never been wet and throbbing for four strangers, no matter how hot they were. Figuring out that my reaction is drug-induced helps to rein it in. I knew it couldn't be natural. "Well, as much as I appreciate the roadside assist, I'd like to leave now."

I step toward the distant sound of civilization, and the group shifts as one to block my escape. Instinct tells me that for every attempt I make to reach freedom, they'll match my movement. I raise my hands and widen my stance.

*Patience. Wait for your moment.*

Riley insisted we take every self-defense class at the community center and practice regularly. It was one thing she never flaked out on. She was militant that we were able to defend ourselves. We usually ended up on the floor in a fit of giggles instead of fending off foes, but still… I'm not helpless.

"Look, I don't want any trouble. Let me be on my way, and we'll forget about this creepy LARPing kidnapping roofie sex trafficking thing you have going on. You do you."

"We didn't roofie you," the bear growls, offended.

"Sex trafficking?" Jaxx snaps, his brow creasing hard. "I rescued you from the side of the road."

"What the fuck is LARPing?" the businessman hawk guy mutters.

Jaxx scrubs a hand through his golden hair. "It's a human game of group dress-up where they prance around with rubber swords and pretend to have powers and abilities."

"Humans are fucked."

"In truth," the young wolf says, pushing his glasses up the bridge of his nose. "Live-action role-play is a creative extension of traditional table-top role-playing games. As far back as the late 70s, participants assumed the identity of their fictional characters to enact a true world adventure either for artistic or dramatic expression."

I pivot my gaze toward him. Is he serious? Did he just barf up a Google search? I scrub a hand over my face and try to breathe. "Forget the LARPing lesson and slow down the crazy train. My point is, I don't care what you boys have going on, I want to leave."

The businessman—Hawk, I think that's what the wolf called him—steps into my personal space and stops a foot in front of me. The intensity of his gaze makes the hair on the nape of my neck stand on end. He's shrewd, alpha dominant, autocratic, emotionally blocked—and sexually aggressive.

How is my body downloading info about him?

His dominance wraps around me. He's horny and hard and the pulsing between my legs picks up to a faster, deeper rhythm. He smells amazing, and, for some reason, my first instinct is to strip him down and see how authoritative this guy is when naked.

I want him to submit to me. *Whoa!* Not sure where the dominatrix impulse is coming from but *hello*. Images of endless pleasures flash through my mind's eye.

Hawk clenches his jaw as the other three groan again. The bear growls and doesn't even try to disguise when he reaches down his jeans to set things right.

"Rein it in, Spitfire," Hawk snaps. While the other three have a sweetness to them, standing this close to Hawk is like running smack into a sexually charged wall of ice you didn't know was there until you hit it.

"This isn't natural," I say, staring into the cold shallows of his gaze. It's shocking, the power of the emotions flooding me. I want him. I need him. The sex will be phenomenal. I know that without question. "You've done something to me, and I want it to stop. Now!"

His gaze narrows. "Your wants became irrelevant the moment you resurrected on the side of that road. Welcome to your second chance at life. Time to get with the program."

I lift my chin and let my anger and need for vengeance take hold. The gaping black hole of Riley's loss consumes me. I am empty. Nothing these men do to me can make things worse. "And what? I'm supposed to accept that I'm a reincarnated mythical bird who rose from the ashes?"

Hawk lifts his palms and I catch sight of one helluva flashy gold watch. I could get thirty large for that sucker. "For reasons we've yet to figure out, something in your DNA triggered a change. Congratulations, you've been reborn an immortal legend of the fae world. By all accounts, that's a shit-ton better than life as a no-mag, nary human."

"You're an asshole."

"No question," he says not missing a beat. "Now, we all need answers, which means we've got a road trip on the horizon. We wasted three days waiting for you to wake up, so let's not waste any more."

"Hawk, step off," the bear says, a deep growl lacing his words. "News flash, big shot. This isn't your boardroom. You're not the CEO here, so give the female a chance to catch her breath."

Hawk casts a dismissive look at the bear, his focus locked on me despite the threat in the other man's voice. A furious growl rips through the air, and tension sparks. How can Hawk ignore the menacing rumble coming from the bear?

Though Hawk stands over six-feet tall, he's still shorter than the bear and not nearly as broad. It isn't his size that makes Mr. CEO intimidating. He's a Type-A alpha with the arrogance of a man used to getting what he wants.

*Annnnd* by the ocular daggers he's shooting me, he wants me to bow down and shut my mouth. Or… maybe bow down and open my mouth.

"Not happening, Christian Grey." I gesture between the five of us and shake my head. "However you imagine this kinky wet dream playing out, you're off-base. I'm outtie."

Hawk's smirk is cold and cruel. "I'm one breath away from testing your resurrection powers once again. You grew up human but try to keep up."

He pokes a hard finger into my sternum. "You—phoenix." He removes his poker and circles the air. "Us—phoenix guardians. The magic of the fae world bound us to you. We are a package deal for the near future, blondie. Destiny has spoken."

My heart pushes at the base of my throat. Whether

it's from what Hawk is saying or the sexual energy pouring out of him and into me, I have no idea.

I choose to believe it's what he is saying.

His brow arches and the look is so hostile and hot my core weeps for a little of his punishment. "Like it or not," he continues, "the five of us are bound. Get over whatever this is: your prudish insecurities, your skepticism, or fear of the big bad men who want to protect you. A phoenix born means trouble is brewing in the magical world. The sooner you stop fighting us, the better it is for all."

# CHAPTER THREE

*Brant*

"So, Mr. Barron," I say, erecting my middle finger and ironically, flipping the bird at the hawk. "May I call you, Mister? Or do you prefer Lord or His Majesty?" My words earn me a glare and a snap of his teeth. "Thanks to your 'get-with-the-program' outburst, our already disoriented mate now thinks the four of us are autocratic stalkers. That's a great start to our relationship."

"Relationship? Don't be naïve, Bear." Hawk is fit, I'll give him that, but he's lived in his ivory tower so long, those muscles are carved by resistance training and DNA, not real-world struggles. He says Calli is unprepared for what's to come. I think that's a pot calling the kettle black situation.

"Like you snapped so brusquely at the female. The five of us are bound."

He chuckles, but there's not an ounce of humor in his tone. "Bound for disaster. Something went wrong somewhere. She isn't even fae."

"She is now," Nakotah says. "The moment her transformation occurred, her body—"

Hawk sends the kid a scathing glare. "She doesn't

have what it takes, kid. That's not blame. It's a simple fact. When word of her existence leaks, members of Darkside will either want to control her or kill her. Even with training, she hasn't got the mettle to fight the battles to come."

"And what? Now you're *psychic*?" I shout. "How about we assess her before you dismiss the wisdom of the fates. Because, despite your ego, the last time I checked, you weren't a god. You're just a mortal male the same as the rest of us."

Hawk shakes his head. "And there's your problem, Bear. On no level are we equals. While you were cleaning out the barn, I was assessing the realities of the fae world and carving out the future of non-humans and our place in this world. No. Whatever wires got crossed with Calli, we need to hightail it to the Bastion and have the elders undo this magical mistake before it's too late."

The thought of asking the elders to sever the bond growing between us knots my bowels. It's offensive—profane. "Whether you acknowledge it or not, whether she fits the mold of the female you would choose or not, Calli is our fifth. Stop undermining her place in our world and get your head out of your tight ass."

"Mark me," Hawk says, holding up his finger. "The first chance she gets, she's in the wind, and we're all fucked."

"So, your answer to that is to drag her across the country, hit veto, and usurp the universe's plan?"

"Damn straight," Hawk snaps, retreating to the corner of the living room. "*We* got cursed being the bonded guardians of a phoenix who is wholly unsuitable. She's a human who holds no skills, and whose first instinct is to cut and run—Yeah, no. I don't fucking think so."

Nakotah frowns and shuts the text he's studying. "She wasn't running away as much as running toward things she understands. This is new to her. Also, I'm unaware of how avians revere the ancestry of our people, but to canines, being summoned as a guardian to the phoenix is a legendary honor."

Hawk barks a laugh. "This isn't the Oscars pup. It's not an honor, to be nominated. That's naivety, not reality. How well do you know women, schoolboy? Do you consider yourself an expert on reading the opposite sex?"

Kotah frowns, and his youthful innocence hardens. "I have a broad base of knowledge through interactions with my sister and her friends."

Hawk points toward the back garden. "That woman is meant to be your mate. That's different than your sister and her friends. How many babes have you bedded in your lifetime? Two? Three? No, I bet my balls you're saving yourself for 'the one,' am I right?"

The look on the pup's face confirms that.

Kotah juts his chin and pushes his glasses up the bridge of his nose. "Statistically, at the age of twenty-one, fifteen percent of males and nineteen percent of females in the United States have yet to engage in sexual intercourse."

Hawk laughs. The guy possesses the personality and warmth of an incoming Arctic ice storm. "Well, sadly, if we don't end this coupling, your chance to pop bottles and bang models is over before it starts. Our libidos are now locked, you get that, right? Our bodies will now respond to one female for the rest of our fucking lives. And that female wants nothing to do with us."

Now it's my turn to laugh. "*That's* what's bothering you? With all the implications of what the arrival of a phoenix means to the fae and human worlds, your concern is that you've been cock-blocked by the universe?"

Hawk glares. "You look like you know your way around women, Bear. You're telling me that you're not pissed to be leashed and bound to just one?"

I shrug. "It's way too early to get wound up about that. And it's not *one* lover—there are five of us. There are lots of possibilities for entertainment there. As Calli said, we're all very pretty."

Hawk's gaze narrows, and he lifts a finger to point at me. "That shit ain't happening. I don't roll that way."

I laugh at the shock on his face. Mr. Know-it-all-Alpha-Millionaire hasn't thought of the different sexual combinations? That suggests he isn't as open and confident as he thinks himself to be. No. It's not shock—it's vehemence. "What? You've never had more than one in your bed?"

"More than one *female*, of course. No males."

I laugh again. "Suit yourself. According to what the kid dug up in the history books, a phoenix draws strength from her lovers and is greedy and passionate. If it takes four of us to satisfy her, I don't imagine it will always be one-on-one."

Hawk stabs me with a piercing glare. "I don't share, and I don't swing. Not. Happening. It's moot anyway because no way will she hang around long enough for your warped little fantasy. That girl is a runner. We need to lock her down and take her to the Bastion before she's a ghost and we're left limp-cocked failures in the eyes of every fae on the planet."

Kotah frowns. "Do you even know if it's possible to break the bond? I haven't come across anything that suggests it's negotiable in any way."

Hawk shrugs. "It's worth a shot. And giving her a possible out is the best way to keep her close until we figure out this mess. State expectations, Bear. It saves everyone the guesswork."

*Jaxx*

*Frickety-frack.* As we sit on opposite sides of the gazebo, I stare at Calli, and my heart aches for her. Our first meeting didn't go at all how I hoped. With no previous exposure to the magic of the fae world, four wildling men chasing her down and shifting in front of her was bound to shock her into withdrawal. Sitting on the edge of the bench, she's tense and ready to bolt at a second's notice. The polar opposite of how I want her to feel.

Well, what's done is done. Lettin' the cat outta the bag is a whole lot easier than puttin' it back in. It's a shame, is all.

When I bonded with her three days ago, she was unconscious. I thought my need to protect her was strong then, now it's overwhelming. Since we only met twenty minutes ago, I have to tread carefully, show her that she's safe.

But even with mistrust radiating from her and her expression tight, all I can think is—*damn* she's beautiful.

I'm a goner.

Her skin is radiant, smooth perfection, and her wide eyes sparkle in the most brilliant hue of emerald green imaginable. Her lush golden hair plays a fiery dance with the morning sun, a hint of her fiery side coming through in russet highlights as it catches the breeze.

The pull of our mating bond tingles in my bones, and by the flare of her pupils and her drugging scent, it's not all one-sided. I can almost taste her arousal in the air, hot with the most intense feminine spice.

Blondes are my preference, true, but Calliope Tannis is more than an attractive package. Liquid fire flares in those emerald eyes with a wildness that calls to my jungle blood. Whether the pull I feel is our bond or me being naturally captivated by her, I may never know. I don't care.

Leaning forward, I rest my elbows on my knees and search for the words that might make this right for her. "Calli, I'm sure your mind is spinnin'. The four of us grew up in this world and had days to come to terms with what happened—you've had less than an hour."

Her head lifts as if she might comment, and then she dips her chin in agreement. I let my FCO psychology field training come forward. This situation isn't all that different from approaching a trauma victim in crisis. "There's no rush or need for you to say anythin', but if you have questions, I'll do my best to answer them. I'm here for you, whatever you need."

She licks her upper lip, and I'm instantly hard at the glossy swipe of that pink tongue. Damn it. I shift on the bench. Such a bastard.

"Can we walk?" she points to the gardens, and her

expression grows guarded as she awaits my response.

"You honestly aren't our prisoner, Calli."

"My mistake." She folds her arms over her ample chest and it makes the swells push at the neck of her t-shirt. "I thought the four of you stopped me from leaving."

I lift my gaze and focus on staring only at her eyes. "Only temporarily, and only for your protection."

She cuts me with an expression that screams of disbelief. "I protect me just fine. Always have, always will. I don't need anyone doing me favors."

The lonely echo within her words makes my cat roar. That she doesn't realize the hollowness of that existence makes me sad for her. Felines are pride animals, members of something larger. I live alone and do my own thing, but I have Leo and my pride at my back at all times.

Who's in Calli's pride?

"My point is, now you don't have to take on the world alone. We're a team."

Her head tips to the side and the dappled light of the sun penetrating the trees strokes the elegant line of her cheekbone. "I didn't ask for a team."

I shrug. "You can put your boots in the oven but that don't make them biscuits."

She blinks at me. "Sorry, I forgot my decoder ring."

"It means, no matter what you want, you can't change what *is*. We're fated. A predetermined bonding of strengths. A collaboration of parts for the strongest whole."

"In your world, maybe. In my world, *I* decide who

I'm with and where I go. You can't say I'm bound to you four as this mythical savior and expect me to shrug and say, 'Yeah, okay. I wasn't doing much with my life anyway. Sure, let's be a fivesome and save the world."

I see her point—it's moot—but I see it.

I feel the rightness of our bonding to the depth of my soul. Why doesn't she? One look at her on the side of that road, and I locked in for the long haul.

Maybe the guardian call works differently on her. She was a no-mag nary. For us, the moment Calli resurrected, fae magic made its selection, and the four of us answered the call.

There was no question.

Maybe being human changes how the pull works. Maybe her cells don't ring with the need to make this work. Maybe she could say no. For the first time, my confidence wavers.

Is that possible? Can she deny her calling? Can she deny us? A cold panic takes root in my gut. What then?

"So, tell me," she says, oblivious to my mental tailspin. "Explain who you think I am now and what that means."

Where to start? Daddy always says, begin at the beginning. "Wildlings and other fae races aren't native to the human realm. Our ancestors immigrated here through portals connectin' this world to a magical realm called StoneHaven. It's a long-established, symbiotic co-existence the humans know nothing about."

Calli and I stroll at a leisurely pace, and I'm pleased to have her attention. As we gain a rhythm, the acidic burn of her anxiety eases, and my gut unknots a little.

"Over time, the wielders of power conflicted with one another. StoneHaven has many races of magical beings, wildlings, mages, trolls, elves, goblins, etc., and eventually, the chaos of rising ambition plunged our home realm into war. The most powerful families of the different races claimed dominion over sectors of StoneHaven and the inhabitants who resided there."

"Evil is as evil does," she says. "I guess it's the same in any realm—human or fae."

I nod. "Several of these families allied and decided that instead of fightin' against other magical beings for a half-destroyed home-world, it would be easier to come here and take over the narys."

"Narys?"

"Yeah. Early settlers found humans ordi*nary*, possessin' *nary* a lick of magic. That's largely the mindset still, though many of us live and work with humans and appreciate them for the strengths they do possess."

"So, your fae ancestors planned to conquer the lowly humans with their magical supremacy. That didn't happen, or I would've known about this before today."

I stop at the fork of two walkways to allow her to choose our path to give her some control over the situation. "Right. When the elders discovered the invasion plan of Darkside—that's what the alliance of the potential invaders was called—the leaders ordered the portals destroyed, and the access points sealed and spelled shut."

I swing back the iron gate that keeps rabbits and deer from nibbling on Leo's garden bounty. More than a garden, the place resembles the hanging gardens of

Babylon. Lush vines drape heavily, burdened with heavy blooms.

The scents of the garden mix with the natural fragrance of Calli's skin—it's succulent.

"I hear a *but* coming."

"*But*, the abrupt finality of the decision to cut off access between worlds stirred up a hornet's nest of opposition and panic. There wasn't time to evacuate and many members of StoneHaven had settled down and mated humans. It was suspected there were Darkside supporters here. There were innocents there. It was a genuine cluster-frackin' disaster."

"And the people stuck here had no access to their ancestral lands or family members left behind?"

"No. And no one knew if the loss of connection to StoneHaven and source magic would cause a loss of magical ability for those trapped here."

Calli sighs. "But what does this have to do with me?"

I stop beneath an apple tree and pick one of the bright red globes. After polishing it on my shirt, I offer it to her.

She declines.

"Wildlings are the protectors of the fae realm, the warrior species that police the races. It is our number one tenet that fae live peacefully with humans and therefore, our existence largely remains a secret. Wildlings ensure that."

"And you think I'm one of those? A wildling?"

"At the time of the portal closures, through a level of magic way above my paygrade, the Elder Council invited the chief mage from each of the four strongest wildling races to come together and spawn a new type of species. Legend states that a phoenix would rise to open the portal door between the worlds if ever the need arose."

"So I'm a mythological key?"

"Legend states that when she rises, the most uniquely suited males belonging to the original four wildling species—feline, canine, ursine, and avian—will feel the pull of the call to their queen. The five are destined to create a powerful quint of magical mates."

She frowns. "Please, don't call us that."

I swallow and try not to show how her rejection cuts. "The magic of our bonding triggered the moment you resurrected. The four of us are here to support you, to defend you, and eventually become more." I hold up my hands when she glares. "When and if *you* decide and not a second before."

Calli pauses in front of a stack of downed limbs collected after the windstorm two nights ago. When she looks up at me, the worry and confusion in her gaze doubles. "Even if I believed any of this, the mating thing is ridiculous. I have a crappy track record with men. I've never made it work with one guy for more than a few months. Four is crazy. I'm temperamental and mouthy and demanding and—"

"—now, you have four males dedicated to meeting your needs, ensuring your safety, and devoted to helping you in the trials to come. Focus on us uniting two worlds not us coming together physically."

She arches a golden brow and even I admit that sounded half-hearted and lame.

"How about this… the more *important* thing to focus on is us growin' into a united force to take on what is to come."

She doesn't look convinced.

"Try somethin' with me," I say.

She stiffens, and a low growl rumbles in the back of my throat. Her tension is driving my animal side into a pacing frenzy. I raise my hands. "I don't mean to push. I only want to show you what it feels like to touch one of your guardians—to simply connect. There's a tether between us and it's growin' stronger every day. Can you feel it?"

She reaches up to pull her hair away from her face. The movement shifts her weight and widens the gap between her t-shirt and the waistband of her yoga pants. Exposed for my appreciation, I take in the lush curves of her hips and the delicate navel piercing I admired three days ago.

*Good gracious, she's beautiful.*

Suddenly, the air in the garden is thicker, hotter, and the space between us is charged beyond electricity. I raise my hands and advance one step. Calli's eyes widen, and I hate the mistrust flaring in her eyes. "I won't hurt you, Calli. Search your instincts… you must feel that."

I wait, hoping she'll mirror my hands and complete the connection. She makes no move to humor me. I want to set up house inside her heart, to be part of her and make her part of me, but she isn't there. That's okay. We've got time.

My cat prowls inside me, eager for what is to come.

I am the chosen mate of the phoenix. How surreal is

that?

*Calli*

I'm diving into the glistening pools of Jaxx's turquoise eyes and can't deny the sexual energy arching between us. Even without touching hands, awareness of him warms my skin. I'm struck by the promise of safety I see burning in his gaze.

For a brief moment, I imagine what it would be like to belong there. What if there is safe harbor from a life that's been cold and hard too long? What if someone else could hold back the world long enough for me to catch my breath?

It's *not* natural.

I drop my gaze.

Jaxx radiates a level of magnetism that has me shifting my legs to ease the tension. The moment I focus on him and the growing connection between us, my cells fire to life, responding to a silent demand my body seems instinctively attuned to answer.

*Go ahead,* a destructive voice whispers in my head. *Meet his palms and connect skin-to-skin.*

I choke the groan that almost escapes my throat. I don't want this. I *don't.* I repeat the words in my head, and wonder—who I'm trying to convince. Standing here with him, I've never felt so free, yet I'm trapped in a dream.

No. It's a nightmare—a twisted, psychological thriller.

Jaxx swallows and his Adam's apple works the smooth column of his neck. His skin glows with a beautiful golden tan, and he smells like fresh air and spruce trees. What would it feel like to press my lips against his throat or, better yet, have him press his lips to mine? My nipples peak as a rush of wet heat dampens my panties.

This isn't natural. It's *not* real.

Fated mates? *Yeah, right.*

I shake myself inwardly. I am drugged or suffered head trauma when I vaulted out my windshield. Whatever the reason, I'm not a reincarnated master key to a magical door to a forgotten realm. I am Calli Tannis, klutzy screw-up, scrappy survivor, and loyal friend to Riley—

Riley—the girl who needs me to avenge her murder and stop the spread of her killers' evil plague.

Turning away, I catch the flash of Jaxx's disappointment. He forces a playful smile and tries to appear unaffected, but the weight of rejection squeezes my lungs.

"Is phoenix the only answer? Aren't there other fae who can resurrect that I could be?"

Jaxx tilts his head side to side. "Not with the way you came back. Calli, you literally exploded into a ball of fire."

"But not impossible, right? What are the other choices?"

"Well… wraith, ghouls, and banshees are undead. And a mage with an undead spell could come back. Or there's a rare cast of pixies in StoneHaven that were said to have the blood of the Fates. I suppose they could resurrect but there are none in the human realm."

I shake my head. “No, like people who were human and then come back.”

He shrugs looking sympathetic. “Phoenix is the only answer, Calli. It’s not what you want to hear, but it is what it is.”

I occupy myself by tossing a few thick branches back into the pile of collected wood, my mind racing faster than my pace. When I straighten, I point at the mansion I escaped earlier. “So, this is your house?” My voice isn’t as strong as I’d like. I’m confused and feel vulnerable and alone. It’s not a feeling I enjoy. In truth, I hate it.

Jaxx flashes me a cocky grin. “No. I got a house down a back road with a porch that needs fixin’ and an inside that hasn’t seen much TLC in far too long—nothing suitable for the arrival of a phoenix. This safehouse belongs to my pride. When I told my Alpha what happened, he invited us here to await the others.”

The others—right, my three other super sexy, paranormal animal shifter mates. Natch.

“And you were sure they’d come?”

He shrugs. “Not a hundred percent, no. Legend said so, and then, one by one, they did. They weren’t sure why they came, only that they were drawn and needed to be here. Once they saw you, like me, they knew.”

“Let’s say I believe you.” I fall back to the two seasons I worked landscaping and burn off some pent-up energy with branch cleanup. “Okay, let’s say I believe that I was reborn due to some dire need of the magical world. Once that’s cleared up, do I go back to being me?”

Jaxx possesses the sleek musculature of his jaguar and the grace and playful demeanor of a cat. When he looks at me, that falls away, and his smile grows serious. "This is forever, Calli. This you *is* the new you. You are reborn."

My chest tightens. I was afraid he'd say that.

He leans into my line of vision and smiles. "On the bright side. You're alive. Without the resurrection, you wouldn't be. There's got to be a reason, right? Some unfinished business the universe wants you to take care of?"

*Yeah*, to avenge Riley, not jaunt off on a magical quest.

My stomach growls and Jaxx shoulder-bumps me toward the house. "Let's see what Brant is fixin' in the kitchen. You slept for three days solid. I bet you're as hungry as our bear. I tell ya. That boy can pack it away."

I tighten my resolve at the same time as I tighten my grip on the branch in my hand. When Jaxx turns toward the house, I swing with everything I have.

He grunts and crumbles to the ground. The tang of blood singes my nostrils and I drop the makeshift club. Oh, gawd. He falls so still, my stomach lurches. If I had anything in it, I might throw up. He's just out cold. He has to be.

I assure myself of that and tear my gaze from the carnage. He seems like a decent guy, but hello—Stockholm Syndrome. Guilt makes my insides squirm, but I push it down.

I run like never before. I have to. They'll come after me, and as Jaxx said, I came back for a reason.

# CHAPTER FOUR

*Calli*

I run across toward the back of the property, my bare feet eating the manicured lawn as I close the distance between me and the sounds of traffic. When I break through the bushes, I stop dead at the perimeter fence to take in my surroundings. Despite hearing cars clearly, we are farther from the road than I thought. I still have a long way to go, and my tender tootsies will pay the price.

Oh well, not my first swim in shit's creek.

Grabbing the top of the wooden fence, I pull myself up. Climbing over is less awkward than I expect, and I flip gracefully to the other side. After brushing off my hands, I leave the landscaped safehouse property of Jaxx's Alpha and head across the wild Texas terrain.

If those guys really are fae shifters, their animals will track me if I stay on foot, but maybe not if I catch a ride. I hop a log and try to evade the thorny bushes. Geez, hostile plants grow wild in every direction in Texas. They claw at my legs and arms, greenbriers and cacti and—crap—does everything growing here have burrs and thorns?

I try not to think about snakes.

Texas has a lot of snakes.

The midday sun beats down on me, and I'm sweated through by the time I reach the strip of asphalt leading to my escape. Ignoring the searing on the bottom of my aching feet, I wave down the first vehicle I see—a bright blue Toyota Tacoma. Climbing up into the passenger side of the truck, I am doubly relieved. First, the rush of chilled air blowing at me from my vents is heaven. Second, I meet the concerned gaze of a woman driver. "Where ya headed, hon?"

I clutch my purse in my lap. "Anywhere but here."

"That I can do." The silver-haired cowgirl puts it in gear, and the pull of the engine getting us moving eases my nerves. A few miles down the road, she turns down the radio and smiles over. "I'm Grace, by the by. I notice yer a little shy in the shoe department. You in some kinda trouble?"

I stare at the scenery as we drive. It isn't exactly a cookie-cutter community, but it's weird how mundane it feels after everything that's happened. Had words like mundane mattered to me yesterday… or three days ago?

Am I different from the girl who crashed into a pole fleeing from the bikers who killed her best friend?

I search the empty road stretching behind us in the side view mirror, and my belly tightens. Jaxx rescued me from a ditch, and I betrayed him. Guilt and regret twist my insides.

Something wild inside me claws to return to them.

Is that real? Is it because I'm drugged? If they drugged me, the effects would've worn off by now, wouldn't they?

Then why do I still feel so drawn to four strangers? The bloody image of Jaxx lying in the forest is burned into my mind's eye. He was sweet to me, and I betrayed his trust.

I swallow hard and clench my fists. Why the hell am I second-guessing myself? They kidnapped me.

They wanted me to have sex with them.

*Four* of them. How does that even work? Would they want me one after the other, all at once? Or did they think we'd set a schedule for different nights of the week? I can't wrap my head around that.

Yes, they are hot—okay, beyond hot—but four?

"I know that look," Grace says, from the driver's seat. "That's man trouble if I ever laid eyes on it. What did he do, darlin'—cheat ye, get rough, take ye for a ride?"

The emotion building in my chest is crazy. I met those four only an hour ago, and here I sit, teeth clenched and with a searing pain in my lungs where oxygen is supposed to be. "I honestly don't know what happened. I'm… confused."

Grace nods and clicks on her indicator before changing lanes. "Been there, got the scars on my ole ticker to prove it. Don't fret, hon. You're as pretty as a speckled pup. If that guy back there isn't the one, there will be three more down the road waitin' on ye, guaranteed."

"That's what I'm afraid of." Shifting my gaze from the road behind me to the front window, I watch the sun burn high above the horizon. "Where are you going?"

"To the Feed & Seed on the township line. There's a

truck stop up the road a spell. I can drop ye there if you like. Maybe a kind-hearted soul hauling a load can help you get to where you're headed."

I nod, squeezing my purse in my lap. Riley died because she poked too deep into Sonny's illegal businesses. It can't be for nothing. I'll take the address, find that property, and figure out everything else after that. "A truck stop will be perfect. Thanks."

*Hawk*

I ride the upswell of the highway thermal, my mind and body roiling with a fury I rarely let myself feel. Our little phoenix is running—*again.* The fact that the other three didn't see who she is doesn't just baffle me—it pisses me off. The four of us are hitched to a runaway train, and they are too legend-struck or cock-dizzy to see our situation as the total derailed wreck it is about to become. *Runners run. That's a fact.*

Was I surprised to find golden boy beaned and bleeding in the garden and our phoenix nowhere to be found? Nope.

I considered helping the brother out, but Calli is more important by far. Without her, we are screwed—or *not*—as the case may be. Still, I hope the whistle I let loose reached the ears of the others, and Jaxx is being tended to.

The damage looked extreme. The jaguar will come out of this with a concussion at best, likely brain trauma.

Sucks to be him. Trusting fool.

I, however, don't share that weakness. The chief factors of my jet-setting success in business are keen instincts, being able to read people and situations, and not allowing myself to be infected with feelings. Emotion muddies the waters—in business and relationships—making things more complicated than they need to be.

Hard truth. In the end, everyone watches out for themselves. I choose me, first and foremost, and am not surprised when other people do the same.

After fifteen minutes of trailing the blue Tacoma toward the next town, it pulls over to a roadside truck stop. Calli hops down from the passenger's seat, waves a friendly goodbye, and heads inside.

Landing on a light standard in the parking lot, I adjust my feathers and fold my wings. I've got a clear view through the diner window as Calli accepts a booth and settles in. I consider shifting back and calling the bear to tell him where we are. That would be the considerate 'mate' thing to do.

Fuck it. No one ever accused me of being considerate.

Calli is hell-bent on ditching us. Forcing her back into protective custody won't solve anything. Maybe I can learn more about her by watching her out in the wild. I am, after all, an expert on assessing people's motivations and figuring out what makes them tick.

A seagull hovers in front of me. It *squawks* and looks like it might land on the light housing next to me. Seriously, there are twenty other lights to land on, what the fuck makes it think it needs to share mine? I flip out a wing and snap the fucker in the breast feathers, knocking it flying.

I turn my attention back to the diner window. I'm

not starting at square one with our mystery girl like the others. I had a preliminary report on her twelve hours after the golden boy showed me into Calli's room, and my mating bond locked into place. So far, I know she's:

- the only child of William and Brittany Tannis,
- orphaned at twelve when her parents died in a house fire
- sent to live with an aunt in Northern California,
- took off at fifteen and on her own ever since
- she's lived in Yuma, Tucson, El Paso, and the list goes on

The survivor in me respects that she's taken care of herself for a decade. The pragmatist in me is disappointed she hasn't raised the bar to better her circumstance.

I did. Street smarts gave me a cutting edge in business.

What has it given Calli?

*Kotah*

The Feline Alpha's library in the safehouse is a two-story sanctuary with floor to ceiling bookshelves, ladders on rails, and a collection of shifter history and ancient tomes that steals my breath. Books are my passion. My father—the Fae Prime—has a library almost twice this size, but when it became apparent that I was more interested in becoming a scholar than a soldier, he banned me from using it.

The loss hit me like the deprivation of the very oxygen that fueled my life's blood.

Mother said that if I proved to Father that I could be

the young male he wanted me to be, he might reverse his order. I trained from dawn until dusk every day after that. My weapons coach said I stood above the rest. My fighting master said he couldn't be prouder.

My father said I'll never measure up.

From outside the royal residence, the Prime sending his male heir away to be educated at the finest schools was perceived as forward-thinking and investing in a future beyond the strength and brutality of our species.

Mother knows the truth. As does my sister, Keyla.

Father is embarrassed by me. Ashamed that I value keen wit more than the keening of swords. Out of sight, out of mind. With me immersed in classes across the country, he pretends the skinny kid who vomits facts when nervous isn't heir to the entire fae world.

Life as a scholar suits me fine. Even with my degrees in ancient studies and anthropology, learning more about how and why people—human and fae—do what they do fascinates me. There is so much to learn from observation.

Now, everything is changing once again.

I am a Guardian of the Phoenix—my duty is to safeguard my mate in whatever challenges brought her into existence.

With my full attention on the wars of StoneHaven and the original closing of the portal gates, it is a wonder I hear the shrill whistle from the garden. The pitch demands my attention and startles me from my studies.

Like any true library, there are no windows near the books, so I leave what I am reading and go out to the balcony at the end of the hall. The moment I sniff the air, the tang of blood calls my wolf.

Launching over the rail, I land on the soft grass at a run. Brant meets me at the gate to the garden, and I don't know what to make of the carnage. Jaxx is bleeding heavily from his head and shifting from jaguar to man and back again in rapid succession. I've never seen anything like it.

"What's happening?"

Brant scowls. "He can't hold his shift. Help me wrap the wound and get him into the house."

"Moving a person with a head injury is ill-advised," I say, assessing the distance from the garden to the house. "We need to look for signs of shock, concussion, or skull fracture."

Brant looks up at me as he points. "Kid, his skull is hanging open. It's very fractured."

*Right.* "In that case, we need to immobilize the patient and call for help immediately. We're in feline territory. Do you know who to call?"

"Yeah, actually, I do." Brant pulls his phone from the pocket of his jeans and dials. "Doc, What's your ETA? I've got an emergency patient. I need you here ASAP."

"You have a doctor friend close enough to help?" Fortuitous. Brant and I spoke a fair bit while Calli remained unconscious. His ursine territory is up the Pacific coastline near Seattle. Not close enough for a Texas house call.

Brant rips his shirt into strips and wraps Jaxx's head. "When Calli wasn't awake by last night, I asked my doctor buddy to come check her out. He caught a flight this morning. He's not far."

Thank the Powers.

"Okay, I've secured his head and will be careful of his neck," Brant says. "Now, will you help me get him into the house?"

I grab Jaxx's legs as Brant wraps his burly arms around the jaguar's chest. As I bend, I track the scent of blood to a long chunk of tree branch lying in the grass beside him. Calli's scent is all over it. "She's running again. Hawk said, she would, and he's right."

Brant growls. "Don't remind me. That arrogant asshole thinks he's got everything figured out. He might be the king in the boardroom, but he has a lot to learn about how to talk to a woman."

The same could be said about me. "Brant, I have no experience in building a relationship. I know nothing beyond biology and social interaction with the females of my pack."

Brant grunts. "Bah. You're a quick study and have that whole sweet and innocent appeal. What you don't know, you're willing to learn. That's very different than an arrogant belief that you've got it all locked down."

That makes me feel a bit better.

My hold dissolves as Jaxx shifts, and we're suddenly carrying a jaguar instead of a man. He hits the ground and, thankfully, his cat is out cold. Wildling animals hate being vulnerable in front of others, and our animals aren't accustomed to one another yet. The last thing we need is for Jaxx's cat to go wild when he's already hurt.

I'm about to ask what we should do, and then the

jaguar shifts back to being Jaxx. Brant and I grapple him again and continue toward the house.

Though I want Jaxx to be well, I wonder how things work. If he dies, is another feline bonded and drawn into our mating, or do we lose one of the species representatives?

There is so much I haven't gleaned yet. Too many questions. "How do you see me fitting in here, Bear?"

Brant looks up as if he's not following.

"Since I realized what the magic call was about, I've wondered how I fit in. What do you think my purpose is as one of the legendary Guardians of the Phoenix?"

"Honestly, I haven't thought that far. If Calli ends up claiming us and accepts her place as our queen, we'll be her lovers and protectors and help her with whatever it is that the future holds."

I know the legend.

What I don't know is who *I* am within the coupling.

Brant is her protector. Jaxx is a strong and steady supporter. Hawk is the shrewd, titan provider. What do I add to the mix? Why did the Fates bestow the canine guardian honor on me? Being the heir to the highest post in the fae hierarchy might be advantageous but it isn't me and I don't want anything to do with it.

Intelligence is what I'm hoping.

It isn't conceited to say I possess a higher than average IQ and attain and retain knowledge quickly and with a great deal of accuracy. Maybe that is my contribution.

"Put him on the floor there." Brant indicates a spot in the living room with the tilt of his head, and I follow his lead. "Shit. Blood is seeping through the wrap. See if you can find some towels we can cut into strips."

"Prop a pillow under his head," I say, chucking a velvety square at him. "And turn his face to the side."

I hustle through the main floor of the feline vacation house, sniffing out the scents of terry and cotton. I find a well-stocked linen closet in the guest bedroom hall. Grabbing a stack, I return and drop to my knees. Holding one of the towels by the end, I pull it taut and hold it out. "Slice this."

Brant releases a wickedly sharp claw from its nailbed and slices the towel down its length. We are almost done rewrapping Jaxx's head wound when he groans. "… Calli?"

"In the wind," Brant says. "Let's worry about you first."

Jaxx tries to push Brant off but gets nowhere. "Find her."

"We will. First, let's get your gray matter back inside your skull. Sound good?"

Brant pulls out his cell and makes a call. "Where the fuck are you? Good. Let yourself in. We're in the living room right of the entrance."

A few moments later, a door swings open with a near-silent swish near the front of the house. I rise to greet the stocky, dark-featured figure in the hall, and sense the ursine in him immediately. I sniff the air. He's a beta, not as big as Brant—no one is—and carries a large medical kit. He also looks intent on reaching his patient.

That's all that matters.

"In here." I gesture the way into the open-concept great room. "He got hit in the head by a heavy branch. He's flipping from cat to man and back again every couple of minutes."

"How long ago was he injured?"

I calculate the time taken from the sound of the whistle to his arrival and take into account how long before that we left Calli in the garden with Jaxx… "I'd say somewhere between twenty-seven and thirty-four minutes."

Doc casts me a look I'm familiar with but doesn't waste time pointing out my oddities. He drops to the hardwood and gets to work.

Once it's obvious Jaxx is in good hands, my priority shifts. "Hawk passed through the garden not long after Jaxx was attacked. My guess is that he's gone after her." The *her* is apparent, and Brant seems to agree with my observation. "We need to join the hunt."

"I'm coming," Jaxx says, rolling to his side.

"No. You need to sit this one out, my man," Brant says.

When Jaxx moves to protest, Brant's doctor friend injects something into Jaxx's neck and the jaguar slumps into unconsciousness. "Go find your mate. I've got him."

"Yeah?" Brant says. "You sure?"

The black bear nods, and we are up and out of the house before I even realize my feet are moving. My mate is upset and out in the world unprotected. We need to find her.

*I* need to find her.

Brant sniffs the bloody branch back out in the

garden. The scent of his anger and frustration wafts on the humid air. "Why did she do this? Why couldn't she believe we want to help her and trust us?"

"Life lessons," I say, following her trail to a point at the fence at the edge of the property. "People who never experience kindness and aid don't trust it when it's offered. Why would they help me? What's in it for them? That sort of thing. With our pheromones sexually heightened, she probably worried about what we wanted in return for our support."

Brant growls. "No one will pressure her into anything as long as I'm around."

"That won't be an issue. From what I've learned about fated mates, and the phoenix guardians in particular, protecting Calli's wants will supersede any of ours. She is our priority. It's woven into the magic of the mating bond."

I lean close to the wood of the fence and inhale. Our phoenix has a very distinct scent, one that is ingrained into my soul. "Go secure us a vehicle," I say, allowing my wolf to prowl forward. "I'll follow her trail and meet you at the road."

As Brant jogs back toward the house, I hop the fence and let each nuance of Calli's scent feed my cells. Emotions hold varied smells: fear, anger, joy, jealousy, love.

Her scent is an enticing mixture of determination, anxiety, the natural pungency of her feminine perfume, and the faint hint of char. It makes sense that her phoenix side is there, but still, I find it intriguing that it's present before she's even shifted form for the first time.

I mull that over in my mind for a bit as I track her

path. By the time I kneel on the opposite side of the road, Brant arrives with—"Isn't this Hawk's vehicle?"

Brant laughs, hanging out the open window of a fully loaded, black beast of a sport utility vehicle. He pulls onto the shoulder, slips it into park, and revs the engine. "This beast seats seven. My truck seats three. I made an executive decision to ensure everyone has a seatbelt on the way home."

*Of course.* Now it was my turn to laugh. "You're stirring up trouble. Plain and simple."

Brant's brow arches in feigned shock. "Hey, building the foundation of a relationship sets a precedent for what's to come. We can't let Mr. Hotshot Hawk get away with his bullshit, or we'll never regain the lost ground. He might be a king of the FCO world, but here he's one-fifth of this mating. No better than any other, despite what he thinks."

"I give you that." Straightening, I round the truck and lean into the passenger window. "Her scent ends on that side. There's nothing over here. Whatever vehicle she got into was traveling west. Unless it crossed lanes to pick her up… No. The likely odds land on her traveling west."

I hop into the truck, and Brant swings us around and hits the gas. "How far behind her do you think we are?"

"By the strength of the scent, I'd say no more than half an hour—perhaps forty-five minutes."

Brant nods, and the engine roars as he guns it. "Well done, kid. Let's go find our mate."

# CHAPTER FIVE

*Calli*

I finish my cheeseburger and swirl a fat beefeater fry in the last of the gelatinous gravy pooling against the inside lip of my plate. Man, starving didn't scratch the surface. Unconscious for three days—that's what Jaxx said. *Jaxx.* I drop the fry and curl my fingers into my palm. As much as I enjoy a heart attack lunch, the food sits heavy in the pit of my stomach. *Jaxx... I'm sorry.*

No. I was right to break free of that destiny craziness. I'm not bound to fae political history like I am to my bestie. Still, part of me longs to see Jaxx's handsome face and ensure he's all right.

*He's not.* I feel it.

But how can I possibly feel it? Despite trying to explain it away, something ties me to those four. It isn't drugs or a head injury. It's something significant that I don't understand.

I wish things went down differently, but don't have the luxury of being sentimental. Sovereign Sons are not the folks to mess with if you haven't got your head on straight. I need to focus, find that property, and figure out how to bring Sonny and his men down.

Pulling my cellphone out of my purse, I turn it on and call up the last address searched. When the map fills my screen my sense of purpose returns. Cool. My car chase and resurrection relocation only took me two hours off course.

I finish the last of my Coke and signal my server over. Brena is a ponytail-pretty brunette who makes jeans and a frilly apron look like they go together. "What can I get you, sugar? Do you want a refill? How about a peek at the dessert menu? We've got fresh pecan pie."

I shake my head. "Working here, you know the regular truckers, right?"

She glances across a sea of heavy-set, ball-capped, rough-cut men. "We have lots of regulars. Why do you ask?"

"I need a ride to Las Cruces. Do you know anyone who makes a run that I can trust to take me for the ride?"

She scans the crowd and purses her lips. "I do—I'd have no problem putting you in the cab with Big Tom or Willie—but neither are here. The boys with regular runs pass through when the roosters are still crowin'. Middle of the day, like this, they're out on the road or on their way back."

"No problem. Thanks. How much do I owe you?"

Brena tears the bill from her order pad and sets it on the table. "Good luck getting to where you're going, girlfriend. Stay safe out there."

That's the idea.

I check the total of my bill and toss twelve dollars onto the table. In the back hall, I find a lost and found bin by the doors to the bathrooms. Snagging a pair of purple sandals, I try not to think about wearing someone else's shoes.

With my prize in hand, I head into the washroom. After I wash up, my reflection in the mirror catches me by surprise. *Wow.* It's the first time I've looked at myself since before the accident. The changes are subtle but noticeable.

My green eyes practically glow emerald now, my blonde hair isn't just flaxen, there are definite strands of copper and gold in there, and the most striking thing is the physical change to my contours. "Where did you girls come from?"

I give my boobs a lift and admire the addition to my curves. My cheekbones seem higher, my lips fuller, my skin a richer tan. "What the hell happened?"

Did I truly die and come back to life?

Am I a reborn magical phoenix risen from the ashes?

I've thought about it a dozen times since Jaxx told me, but how do I believe something like that? Me, a nothing-special girl, dies in a car crash and is reborn as a legendary savior for a realm of magical fae.

Yeah, and if they knew who I am, the fates or destiny or their gods would pull their hands back and say, "Whoops, our bad. Yeah, no, not you. Wrong girl."

Me walking away saves them the trouble.

"Hey, blondie," a man says as I exit the bathroom. Donning grease-stained jeans and a worn plaid shirt, he pushes off the wall like he's waiting for me. "I heard you talking about Las Cruses. I'm heading that way if you want a ride as far as El Paso."

I eye up the man offering the lift, and my creep-o-meter needle flips into the red. "That's kind—and thanks—but it turns out a friend of mine is coming this way. I'm heading out to the parking lot now to meet up with her."

"Suit yourself."

I turn on my heel and exit the back door. I'll walk to New Mexico before I get into a closed cab with that guy. I wait out of sight, watching as my plaid nightmare hauls his fat ass into his rig and starts up the engine. It rumbles and the cab shimmies as stinky black diesel exhaust spits out of the pipes.

Good. That is good. Once he clears out, I'll mill around and see if I can find a ride with someone that doesn't make my skin crawl.

The beefy rumble of Harley engines registers and my heart trips in my chest. I jog around a parked horse trailer to get a better look at the highway. Yep, a dozen choppers ease off the asphalt to slow in front of the diner.

My heart punches at the base of my throat, making it hard to swallow. There are lots of MCs along these highways and no reason to believe these guys are Sovereign Sons.

Ha. Paranoid much? What are the odds?

The leader pulls off his helmet, and his straggly blond hair falls to his shoulders. I sigh. I should never ask questions like that. No matter what life I live the fates seem determined to bite me in the ass. The rest of the group takes off their helmets. Yep, I know them, and sure as shit, they'll know me if they see me. I'm not about to give them a mulligan to kill me a second time.

Only one way to make sure that doesn't happen.

I take my phone out of the side pocket on my purse and slide it into a slot on the horse trailer. The thing clunks to the wooden floor inside and I sigh. If they came for me, it's the only thing that could've been traced.

Now, to get out of here.

Plaid Nightmare's rig jerks as it jostles to life and pulls out of its parking spot. I run up the side of the truck, grab the hand bar, and climb up on the rail. Unlatching the door, I swing up to look over the seat. "Hey, sorry," I say, as he cuts off the gas. "Turns out, my friend got tied up. Is that ride to El Paso still open?"

"Hop in, and we'll find out."

"Thanks." I settle into the passenger's seat of the big rig and keep my shoulders turned away from the diner. Is it a coincidence that the Sons are here? Did they track me? Damn. I want the element of surprise. Do they know I'm not dead?

*Hawk*

What the fuck is the female up to? First, she bolts from the diner looking like her perfect little ass is on fire. Then she hides within the maze of trucks and semis slotted in the parking lot, and then she catches sight of a bunch of gangers and throws herself into a moving vehicle.

Curiosity piqued, I launch off the light standard and drop to the ground behind a poultry truck filled to bursting with clucking chickens. Straightening as a man, I flash on jeans and a leather jacket. With a quick jog, I make it in the side door and up to the counter at the same time as two bikers.

"Coffee, black, to go," I say to the waitress who served Calli. I pull a ten off the outside of my billfold and toss it on the polished Arborite.

"Nice ink." I point to the forearm of one of the guys in leather. By my experience, it doesn't matter who you're talking to, if they have flashy ink, they like it noticed. "How long did you sit?"

The biker, a buzz-cut, square-jawed, roid-droid type pulls up the arm of his T-shirt and exposes one hell of a violent sleeve. "Fifteen hours to lay it. Another six to fill."

I nod, activating the scanning chip on my watch, and reach closer under the guise of examining his tattoo. "Nice. My back took thirty-two over four sittings. Worth it."

The waitress comes back with my order. I dip my chin to take a quick peek at the results of my scan and step to the side to fiddle with the lid of my coffee.

"What can I get y'all?" the waitress asks.

"We're looking for someone. You ever see her in here?"

I cast a casual glance as I turn to leave, and my phoenix mate gets a whole lot more interesting. There are things my intel report hasn't turned up, like why Calli, a woman who's lived her whole life human, is being tracked by a gang of leather-vested drow.

Taking my leave, I step outside and frown. The bond between the other guardian mates and I is intensifying. As much as it pisses me off, their presence rings like an echo in the back of my mind.

They're close and getting closer.

Instead of shifting to track Calli in the semi, I hand my untouched coffee to the homeless guy panning for change and jog out to the road. Hey, what do you know, a large brown and silver wolf is trotting up the graveled shoulder, right in front of my Navigator.

When they get close, I step in front of my truck and give the bear the finger. "You boys are late to the party. Let me fill you in on what you've missed."

*Calli*

With my stomach full of greasy diner food, the adrenaline of my escape from Sonny dying down, and the bouncy sway of my seat in the rig, I start to feel sluggish. Maybe I'm not completely healed from my car accident. Or maybe resurrecting from the dead takes more out of a girl than I realized. Or maybe it's just that the sun is dipping low. Whatever the reason—despite my objection—my eyes grow heavy.

Eventually, they droop closed against the sting of oncoming headlights. I fight sleep, reviewing my options for when I find the Son's property. Will it be an out of the way warehouse where they store illegal guns and drugs? Will it be a holding station for kidnapped and coerced women?

No doubt there will be armed guards stationed to secure the MC's contraband. I need to get in there to confirm there's damning evidence that will cripple them. Then, do I call the cops or take my revenge to the next level? Am I capable of taking Sonny on and ending his life?

The violent image of Riley's body thrown away like garbage fuels the rage burning inside me. Yeah. I think I can. That's assuming I can get that close. Until I know for sure, I can't act. My plan has to be solid if it's going to work.

What if the property isn't where they stash their goods?

The thought of finding myself back at square one makes me nauseous. I'm running out of time… and money. Revenge is expensive. With everything Riley and I have put together, I've got about twenty-two-hundred bucks. I'm willing to spend it all if it means taking down the men who hurt her but it'll run out sooner rather than later.

I have no time to lose. Who knows what's changed in the three days I rested in that safehouse sleigh bed? Maybe it's already too late, and they moved things knowing I want them to pay. With worst-case scenarios spinning in my head, I miss the downshift of the truck engine.

I startle to high alert when the air brakes squelch, and the cab lurches forward to a stop. My eyes pop wide and I cast a sideways glance at the driver. "Why did you stop?"

"Just takin' a piss. Nothing for you to worry about. Give me two and we'll be back in business."

Oh, all right.

Plaid Nightmare swings his door open and drops down and out the truck's cab. I examine the deep purple sky through the windshield and figure we have about ten minutes until full dark. How far are we from El Paso? How long will it take me to get to Las Cruses? It's hard to know without a vehicle to get there… or a phone to map it.

Maybe I should rent a car when we get to—

My door flies open, and rough hands grab hold. Plaid Nightmare unlatches my seatbelt buckle and pulls me out of the truck. My feet scrabble over the gravel as I try to get them under me. He's dragging me too fast to regain my balance.

Heat explodes in my chest as panic thunders through my veins. My scalp screams as he caveman-drags me away from the road. By. My. Hair. I squirm and flail and claw. My scalp is on fire. I try again to get my feet beneath me but can't.

If he thinks he can drag me into the roadside scrub and rape me, he has another thing coming.

My defensive mind catches up. I search my surroundings and look for an opening. This isn't my first rodeo. If he intends to violate me, he'll release his hold to unbuckle my pants. When he does, I'll fight.

I scream for help, but know no one will come.

Riley's voice sounds in my memory. *You are responsible for saving yourself. Always.*

The world tilts as my legs fly out from under me. I land hard on my back. Air rushes from my lungs with violent force as my skull rattles inside my head.

Dizzy and gasping, I miss my opportunity. By the time I can breathe, meaty fingers are delving into my pants.

"I'm going to kill you," I scream, fighting with

everything I have. "You're going to die, asshole."

Fiery rage ignites in my chest and grips me in the guts. It builds in my throat like magma trapped in the blocked funnel of a volcano and drowns out every other rational thought. It pushes up, up, ready to burst.

It's strength. It's danger. It's power.

Heavy weight straddles my hips before a knee drops to my chest. With me pinned, he works his belt loose. The denim of his jeans pushes against my mouth. The stench of old engine grease fills my sinuses. Bile burns the back of my throat.

"I'm going to kill you," I repeat, feeling the certainty of it boiling in my blood. "You *will* die."

A wild beast clamors inside me and merges with my battered soul. It wants out. It wants the freedom to protect me, to fight, to get this asshole off me.

The volcano erupts.

My world explodes with the light of a thousand suns. My fury unleashes, free to do as it intends. Light bursts off my skin with blinding force, and when the filthy pig flies backward, I launch off the ground and lunge.

Now, it's me holding him down, my knee grinding his balls into the ground, my hands around his throat as his skin smokes and he screams for help.

"Scream all you want. I told you how this would end."

I'm lost in my fury but don't regret a thing. There's no remorse… only satisfaction that I *can* take care of myself.

I register the shifting shadows an instant before I'm

knocked on my ass by a silver blast of energy. Pain detonates from my shoulder and crawls through my body like an Arctic tidal wave. I stare at the bloom of an exploded ice bomb as it melts on the torched ground around me.

*Ice bomb?* Hubba-wha?

As the shuffle of footsteps closes in, I spin onto my knees. Sonny and his leather-clad goons position themselves around me. They're the same bunch of low life losers they've always been, but at the same time, they're not. Their faces look long and gaunt, and there's a weird mustard-colored aura surrounding them that sparks and expands as they move.

Warning tingles across the back of my neck.

What the—

"Well, well," Sonny says, stepping beyond the line of trees and into the clearing. Like all the Sons, he has scraggly bleach-blond hair and is built like a brick shithouse: broad in the shoulders, slim waist, all sinew, and muscle. Sonny has the bonus of a scar that pulls his lip up in a creepy smile. "You're full of surprises, Barbie. Didn't we already kill you?"

The heated wildness in me is gone, and the sense of power I had frying the trucker is quickly dissolving. The ball of icy flame that hit me drained my power. I look at the flesh of my palms and the lingering licks of flame flicking from my fingertips.

I'm flaming out.

"I'm not dead. Or at least, not anymore."

Sonny frowns at Blade. "You said she was dead."

He nods. "She must've rezzed, somehow. Explains

the human torch routine we walked in on."

The corner of Sonny's twisted smile pulls up as he approaches. He stops beyond my arm's reach and breathes deep. "How did a worthless nary end up as a phoenix?"

I remain half-crouched. Naked and with my muscles aching, I'm far too vulnerable. My quivering legs feel like rubber beneath my weight. "Diamond in the rough, I guess."

I search the expectant faces of a dozen men I've known in passing since Riley caught Viper's eye six months ago. The anticipation in their dark gazes makes my stomach flip. I fight the revulsion rising within—my survival instincts going berserk. I'm in no shape to outrun these men… or take them on.

"You should've stayed dead, Barbie. It would have hurt less than what's in store for you now."

Snake chuckles. "You gonna let us have her, Boss? Can we see if she fights as good as her little friend?"

There's a murmur of male interest. Fury stings my eyes.

"We'll make sure she suffers," someone shouts from the shadows.

Sonny tilts his head from side to side and then shrugs. "All right. Use her, then kill her. And make sure she stays dead this time. The last thing I need is a phoenix fucking up my plans."

The sweep of his hand toward me signals the start of the main event. His men launch.

Mischief, Sonny's Sergeant at Arms, lunges at me, teeth bared. He goes straight for my jugular. As crazy as a vampire attack seems, my instincts kick in and I manage to save my throat. I don't get away clean, though. Those pointy fangs catch my collarbone and I scream as he bites down.

He doesn't bite long. He curses and tears away, a chunk of my shoulder in his mouth. "Fuck! She's hot."

I fight, struggling against the hold of three men. They are too strong, but my skin is really hot because the stench of burnt flesh singes my nostrils. The stars above spin as I slam down on the scorched grass and hit the ground hard.

I pummel and claw at any flesh I see.

The taste of char burns in my throat, but my heat refuses to ignite. Mischief snaps at me again. I kick at the massive bodies, pinning me down. An elbow slams into my jaw and the world fritzes out of focus.

Panic and pain rush through me.

*Don't pass out.*

I twist and kick my limbs with all my strength. I hear screams. It might be me. I'm nauseous with the smell of burning hair and flesh. They don't hold on long before they curse, and another comes at me.

A hard fist connects with my temple. I groan and the world dims. Agony pierces my other shoulder. I glare as the pain leaches through my body. What kills a phoenix? Am I like a vampire? If so, I'm in big trouble because there's a wooden stake sticking out of my body.

A sharper pain sears my abdomen. I curl my knees up and scream. My scrabbling becomes more desperate than determined. I flinch as my arm is gouged. I try to reach the power inside me, but nothing registers—except pain.

Shouts ring out.

The stink of Mischief's breath floods my sinuses. He draws his hot, wet tongue up my cheek, and I know I've lost. A thunder of rushing footsteps brings another round of men on top of us. Maybe they'll kill me quickly, and I'll come back again and make them pay. *Can* I come back again?

I don't know how resurrection works.

I don't know anything about my powers.

I don't even know what the hell Sonny and his men are.

My fault. I should've listened to Jaxx and the others—

The weight on me vanishes, replaced by warm fur at my hip and a vicious growl and snap of teeth toward the attacking world. I blink past the blood stinging my eyes. My vision is spotty and double, but I feel his presence as clearly as see him. My wolf is here.

He hunches low, his dagger-tipped fangs gleaming in the moonlight. I sink my fingers into the lush coat of my protector and sag to the forest floor.

My wolf… is… here.

# CHAPTER SIX

*Brant*

I barrel through the core of Calli's attackers and take five down in a juggernaut run. It's crude and only works because even in human form, I'm that big. With the added bonus of the element of surprise, I take the win. Calli's down and bleeding bad. I have to hold off these bastards long enough for Kotah to stabilize her. My contribution doesn't have to be pretty, just effective. It's why I'm here for her.

Getting back to my feet, I tip my neck from side to side and roll my shoulders, splitting my t-shirt in the process. "Care to dance, gentlemen? Or do you only fight females?"

Finally, after days of sitting on my hands, I get to stretch my legs. And fists. Yeah, don't forget my fists. After dealing with Hawk's superiority bullshit and worrying about Calli, I'm spoiling for a bloody throwdown.

Heavily weighted odds get the adrenaline pumping.

Pounding these degenerate assholes is what I need to let off some steam and center myself. Nothing cleanses the soul like a good wholesome slaughter. I think Gandhi said that—I snort and piledrive a loser in the face—maybe not.

"Calli! Oh, no. Calli, can you hear me?"

The panic in the kid's voice shifts my world. The kid has shifted and is trying to stop the hemorrhaging. My mate suffers because of these drow scum. They tried to take her from me before we've even begun.

Mind: fractures. Temper: rages. Control: snaps.

As a dozen rush me, a switch flips. I push my claws through the nailbeds of my fingers and Freddie Krueger the fuckers like you read about.

I duck as an ice bolt of frozen magic zings past my ear. Four more move in and flank me from all sides. One grabs my arm while two try to take me to the ground. Screw that.

I ram my claws into the fleshy belly of one and swipe left, hard and fast. As his insides become outsides, I slit the throat of the second, and then nail my hat trick with an uppercut of claws through the guy's chin and up into his skull. That move, I stole straight from Wolverine.

Yep. Life imitating art.

As bodies continue to drop, I get into a mass-murdering groove. Violence flows through me with an ease that might chill a lesser male to the bone.

Me—*nah*—I'm in the zone, baby.

Grabbing the wrist of my last attacker, I spin the guy and twist him into a chokehold. One satisfying crack later and the drow falls to the heap with the others, his head hanging limp.

Hawk's in hand-to-hand magical combat with the

last man standing, and I raise a brow. Magical offensive abilities are beyond rare in the wildling world. What else don't we know about our FCO king of the world?

I file that away for later and check the state of deadness of the fallen. We don't want anyone rallying to get back up. Nope. All dead in a final death sorta way. Nice.

The sound of Harley motors revving at the side of the road highlights the hasty retreat of at least a few of the leather-clad losers. It's too far to get there before they take off, but the important thing is that the good guys won.

Yay, team!

*Kotah*

I press my hands against the gaping tear in Calli's side and try to staunch the bleeding at the base of her neck as well. "One of you, give me something to stop the blood flow!"

Hawk shreds his shirt, yanking it off his shoulders with the brute strength of a mate possessed. He checks that Brant is taking inventory of the dead drow and drops to his knees in the blood-soaked ground beside me. "She'll be fine," he says, pressing the expensive tatters against the damage. "Look. See, her wounds are already starting to heal."

I stare at the carnage, willing him to be right. What does he see that I don't? Hawk always sounds so cocksure and dictatorial it rakes over my nerves like broken glass. This time, I pray he knows as much as he thinks he does.

Calli must be all right. I only just found her and haven't started to get to know her yet. I run my hands over the damage her body sustained. Legend states that phoenix healing powers are incredible. It's not happening fast enough.

Closing my eyes, I use our fledgling connection to grasp the mating bond between us. Yes. I feel it. The avian is right. Calli's injuries are knitting back together.

I try to rid my mind of the horrific images of Calli being beaten by the drow, but the brutality burns in my memory. The three of us raced from the edge of the blast zone as fast as paws and wings could carry us.

Calli was on fire when we arrived—literally on fire.

Thankfully, a hundred feet or more from the road, behind an abandoned shack surrounded by trees, no one could see what was happening. And if they did, they wouldn't believe it.

Even knowing Calli is a phoenix, *I* hardly believe it.

By the Powers, she was magnificent… and then the horde of dark elves attacked from out of nowhere.

"Calli," Brant says, joining us. The bear is huffing, his mighty chest heaving and covered with blood. He's taken a few hits, but, like Hawk and I, is solely focused on our fallen mate. "Kid, tell me she's alive."

"She is," I say, a small shiver of relief passing through me. "But she's been through an ordeal."

I tilt my head toward the trucker lying twenty feet away. He's scorched extra crispy and it doesn't take a Rhode Scholar genius to figure out what brought Calli back here and triggered her shift. The heat of her fury burned a twenty-foot radius of grass and scrub.

Brant growls. "If the filthy piece of shit wasn't dead, I'd rip him to ribbons myself."

I glance at the mangled corpses flung around the clearing and my respect for the bear ratchets up a few notches. For an easy-going rancher turned FCO enforcer, he is well on his way to proving himself a lethal guardian.

I wouldn't want to go up against him.

A throaty moan lets off as Calli tries to squirm from my hold. "Calli, you're safe. It's Nakotah—we've got you."

"My wolf," she whispers, her eyes still closed. She relaxes and brushes my arm with soft fingers.

The gentle smile that graces her lips sends a pulse of heat over my skin and a wave of possession to the animal pacing within me. "Yes, *Chigua*, your wolf."

Yours to claim. Yours to command. Yours to love.

"I hurt Jaxx," she says, her voice choked. "Tell him I'm sorry. I never meant to—"

I pick the blood-matted hair from her cheek and frown. "You can tell him yourself. You're healing. That's all that matters. Rest now."

"I've got cleanup," Hawk says, his voice strained as he pulls out his phone. "You two take Calli back to the house. Once she's cleaned up and well, we'll regroup."

Calli rouses and forces her eyes open. "No. I won't go back to lick my wounds while those animals ship off their guns and get away with killing Riley."

I glance up at the others to see if they know what she's talking about. Brant blinks as blank-faced as I am.

Hawk, however, doesn't miss a beat. He scowls, his

icy, steel-gray eyes growing dark. "You are the priority, Spitfire. Your roommate is already dead. It does her no good for you to sacrifice—"

"No," Calli says, struggling to sit. She winces when she moves and grabs her side. "If the Sovereign Sons are mixed up in your magic shifter world, Riley didn't have a chance. How many other innocent girls will they kill? You don't know these men like I do. They have to be stopped."

"You almost died twice this week trying to avenge her," Hawk snapped. "There's only so much a nary is worth."

Calli clasps my wrist and I understand immediately. I pull her to her feet and hold her steady. She burned off her clothes again. I try to not brush anything too intimate, but she's slick with blood and it's awkward to hold her up.

"Riley may be a worthless human to you, but she was my everything. She had my back from the day she came upon me on the street and I'm not about to repay that by letting those ice-ball wielding freaks in leather get away with it."

"Drow," Brant says. "A race of dark elves known for both their malicious intent and their ruthless disregard for life. I never thought I'd say this, but Hawk is right, beautiful. You going after them is too dangerous. Our job is to protect you, and that means you go back to the feline safehouse."

Hawk offers the bear a quick nod. "That's settled. I'll have my team—"

"Whoa, wait. Nothing is settled." Calli straightens and fights to stand on her own. I release her, remaining at the ready in case she swoons. "I may have lost my say in the turn my life took, but I never signed over my right to make my own decisions. From what I've heard, you work for me. Not the other way around."

Hawk's gaze is scathing, his jaw clenched tight. "How do we protect you if you refuse to stay out of harm's way? If we work for your safety, let us do our fucking job."

She points and a shower of sparks spit off her fingertip. "Your job isn't to pit yourself against me at every turn. Maybe it hasn't sunk in yet, but I don't back down. If we're doing this phoenix thing, it's a partnership not a dictatorship."

The two of them standoff, glaring. Touching her, my gift picks up how difficult it is for Calli to bite back her anger.

Hawk's chest expands on a deep sigh. "Very well, Spitfire. Tell me what you know, and we'll assess the situation."

Calli looks skeptical but relents. "Every six months the Sovereign Sons sell a shipment of girls and guns to some rich asshole who calls himself the Black Knight."

Hawk stiffens, his gaze dark and volatile. "And what do you know about this Black Knight?"

"Nothing, really. Riley overheard Sonny's guys talking in the bar where she worked. She went to the cops and they did nothing. They wanted more than drunken chatter in a bar. They said that if she came to them with something they could use, they would look into it. She got friendly with the patched members to find out more. Sonny must've figured that out because they brutalized her, killed her, and dumped her in an alley like garbage."

"And that's horrible for both of you," Hawk says, his frown harsh. "I run a policing agency that takes care of things like this. If drow are affecting human lives negatively, that falls within FCO jurisdiction. There's no need for you to put yourself into the crosshairs. I'll put together a task force and take them down."

"When? Next week? Next month? No. They know I'm alive. They know I'm coming for them. Tomorrow they'll be in the wind and the girls they have will be lost. Riley died trying to stop that from happening. I'm going after the Sons. You can come with me or not, but there's no scenario where I go back to a safehouse and wait."

Hawk stiffens as if an invisible rod rammed up his posterior. "No matter how determined you are, you won't be engaging in a battle with the drow. You are ill-equipped to defend yourself and too valuable to place in harm's way."

I agree with Hawk, but don't speak out. The last thing Calli needs is for everyone to gang up on her. She needs an ally. "What if you oversee from nearby?" I suggest. "Allow Hawk's team or us to handle the confrontation with the drow and you remain at a safe distance."

She wets her lips and swallows as if she's still in pain. "No. I need to go. Riley was my friend. I want to be the one to end Sonny's reign."

"Calli," Brant starts, but Hawk breaks in.

"Tell me, sweet cheeks, do you plan to confront a horde of hostile drow naked? When you resurrected, your skin didn't cool enough for clothes for three days. Will you swagger in alongside my men with your perky breasts swaying and your core exposed for all to see? I don't fucking think so."

I draw in a tight breath as Hawk's eye flash gold and his animal surfaces. Even if we, as men, can pull off civility in this mating madness, our animals are possessive and protective beyond reason. The ferruginous hawk is the largest and most lethal of his species. Hawk is an aggressive and high-profile alpha male. Understandably, Calli's suggestion pushes his limits.

The magical tension in the air is palpable. Hawk is fighting to keep his form. I can't blame him. If my wolf had his way, I'd lay Calli on a cushioned pallet of silk and wrap myself around her forever.

"It's likely moot anyway," Brant says, holding up his large hands. "That was the first time you connected with your phoenix and shifted."

Hawk snorts. "It was a partial shift at best. A true phoenix is fifteen feet tall and has a flaming wingspan of almost thirty feet."

"Where the fuck is your remote, so I can mute you," Brant snaps. "For a first shift, she held her form longer than anyone I've ever seen. For fuck's sake she transitioned three days ago."

"What does that have to do with me going after Sonny?"

Brant smiles at Calli. "Aren't you exhausted? I slept for two days after my first shift. Most wildlings do."

"No," Calli says, shaking off Brant's concern. "I'm fine and I'm going after Sonny. End. Of."

Calli and Hawk remain locked in a glare of wills.

Brant looks as if he's run out of ideas. I open my mouth and hesitate… but no, I'm the omega in this group. Maybe it's my purpose to calm the waters.

"A compromise," I suggest. "Together we follow Calli's direction and assess the danger. If there is a way to allow her closure, we escort her in and get out of there as quickly as possible. If there is imminent preternatural trouble, Calli will trust those better equipped to handle the drow and remain well out of harm's way."

The deadlock of the power struggle fizzles out as Calli releases her fists. "Fine. I'll accept that."

The others might not be close enough to smell the lie, but I do. Our phoenix isn't content to sit on the sidelines.

"You're too stubborn for your own good," Hawk snaps. "You know nothing of the dangers of our world, you're untrained, and if you die, what happens to us?"

An icy shiver runs the length of my spine at the thought.

Calli juts her chin. "I get that you don't think much of me, but if I'm supposed to be a fae savior, I won't start out by hiding while others fight my battles. You don't know me yet, but no one fights my battles except me."

## CHAPTER SEVEN

*Calli*

For the second time in two days, I wake in a strange place, naked, and wrapped in the fire blanket. This time, though, I'm in a moving vehicle and remember most of what happened. It isn't a clear memory of something I did, more like a distant record of events, detached from me. A movie playback of scenes I watched a week or two ago. It was me, but not me.

It's enough to make it clear that whatever threshold I crossed when I resurrected as a phoenix, there is no going back. My new normal is bizarre and dangerous and—not all bad—filled with sexy, great-smelling men.

They need to realize I run my own life, though.

"Hey, you're awake," the young wolf says, smiling down at me as I drool on his collared shirt. The two of us are in the middle bench seat of Hawk's SUV, with the bear snoring in the shotgun seat and Hawk driving. "How are you feeling?"

I push up and swipe a hand across my cheek to dry my face. "Like my life got hijacked and now everyone thinks they have a say in who I am and what I do." He flinches and I regret the snark. "Sorry. I'm cranky."

Kotah shrugs but it's obvious I hit a nerve.

"How long until we get to the address I gave you?"

Hawk meets my gaze in the reflection of the rear-view mirror and fragments of our standoff last night drift into my mind. "An hour, maybe an hour and ten. I'll pull over beforehand so we can wake up and stretch. Then, I'll fly ahead and see what we're dealing with. My recon team arrived there half an hour ago and are assessing the scene. They are trained and capable to handle this."

"But they'll wait until we arrive, right?"

The look Hawk shoots me is too raw for my comfort. He doesn't like me. And more than that, he doesn't like that I refuse to let him set the rules of my life.

Tough titty.

A soothing touch on my arm accompanies a wave of soothing energy. "Your shoulders healed nicely."

I turn my attention back to Kotah and follow his gaze to the rounds of my shoulders. He's right. The damage done by Mischief's bite and the wooden spike are both healed with no trace that I was ever hurt. "How is that possible?"

"Phoenix have unprecedented healing abilities," Kotah says, his gaze is reverent. I catch him staring and his gaze jerks away as his cheeks flush. "You are very special."

My wolf has a kind soul and a gentle air. His hair wafts in the breeze from the open window and it's like he's posing for an erotic male model magazine. But better—live and in person—I can smell, touch, and maybe even taste him. Shifting back to where I woke against his shoulder, I inhale deeply and pull his earthy forest scent deep into my lungs.

My cells expand and burst awake inside me. "Thank you for supporting me back there. I… uh, appreciate you trying to find a compromising solution."

He dips his chin. "I'm sorry about your friend. It sounds like she was brave and driven, like you. I'm sure the two of you together were quite a force to be reckoned with."

I stare out the deeply tinted window and sigh. "Riley was stubborn and fun and crazy and impossible to predict. She lived every moment like it was a precious gift."

"It takes a great deal of courage to live like that."

He's right. Riley was fearless. If I was more like her, sitting here next to Kotah, I wouldn't hold back.

Riley never held back.

I'm so incredibly drawn to him. I yearn to brush a hand down the side of his face. His copper skin looks warm and inviting like it was kissed by a sun god. His features are strong and regal yet, of the four of them, he seems the most self-deprecating. He's a delightful mystery.

Despite him looking like a college junior, he hasn't once acted or spoken like a kid. He seems to have a wise old soul. Several times, I've noticed the others pose a question and turn to him as if expecting him to hold the answers.

"What were you saying to me, last night?" I ask, straightening in my seat. I stop refusing my need for a connection of skin-to-skin and drop my hand toward his.

The second our fingers twine, a zing of pure need rushes through me and takes root in my heart.

Jaxx was right. Simply touching brings the rightness of our connection into reality. Poor Jaxx. It sickens me that I hurt him, that I refused this connection with him, that I betrayed his trust and left him bleeding all alone.

I swallow and push that into the 'fix later' pile. Right here and right now, I need to focus on something positive. "You were speaking to me while I dozed off a few hours ago, but I didn't understand the words."

Kotah ducks his head and pushes his glasses up the bridge of his nose. "I recited what I remember of the legend of the phoenix. It's a story the children of my nation hear around the fire at equinox celebrations. You are a living symbol of inspiration. The arrival of the phoenix signals the possibility of uniting StoneHaven with those living here with the humans—a reconnection with our ancestry and inherent powers."

How's a girl supposed to respond to that?

"Wanna hear something crazy?"

Kotah cants his head to the side as if considering it.

The gesture is very canine and makes me smile. "When I died, I wasn't scared. I crashed through the windshield and shattered my insides when I hit the road. I laid in that ditch, knowing I would die, and wasn't afraid. Could I have known on some level what was coming? Is that possible?"

He shrugs. "I'm sorry. There's so much we don't know."

"And why me?"

He blinks owlishly, studying me from behind his

lenses. "Alignment of the stars, a Fate's guiding hand, a random occurrence. We may never know that either. The point is, that you *are* here. You are with us, as you are meant to be. You must not run off again. That was very dangerous."

"Can you blame me? I woke up locked in a mansion with four men telling me we're some cosmic mating-match."

Kotah frowns. "We didn't lock you up. Jaxx ensured your room and balcony doors were free to open. We only wanted to escort you through the early days of transition. If you told us about your friend and the men who hurt you, we might've been able to help without the bloodshed and pain. We are your guardians, first and foremost, here to serve you."

It's hard to deny the phoenix thing—especially with last night's trucker bonfire drifting in and out of my memory and the taste of my blood lingering sour on the back of my tongue.

What is so bad about being reborn a magical being?

Jaxx was right about another point, too. If I were dead, none of this would matter. Riley would still be dead, and Sonny and his guys would get away with it. So what if I can't go back to my life as a human?

Do I even want to?

As crazy as the concept seemed yesterday, I take a page out of Riley's book and I allow myself to consider the four of them and what they represent. The changes in me aren't solely sexual. The boundaries of my life are expanding and I am grasping to catch up.

They didn't drug me—I get that now. And though

I'm not sure what happens after I bring down the Sons, I acknowledge things aren't as absolute as I thought.

Kotah watches me, patient and reflective. I'm struck again by his youthful energy. "How old are you?"

He purses his lips and I feel his guard go up. "I'll be twenty-one on my next birthday."

Twenty. Gawd. He's not even old enough to drink in a bar and he's been chosen as one of the Guardians of the Phoenix. I give him full marks for maturity. He's handling things with far more grace than I. "Are you angry… having your world flipped upside down and being locked into this craziness as one of my men?"

His guarded expression drains away. "No. I am honored and…" a hint of a smirk plays at the corners of his mouth as he smiles at our joined fingers, "honestly, I worry the Powers will realize they've chosen the wrong male, and that at any moment they could take it all away. I can't imagine finding anyone as strong and beautiful as you. I don't understand how I deserve a place at your side."

My cheeks flush and I try to clear my head and find my tongue. "That's sweet."

"It's true. I will do anything for you, Calli, be anything you need: a protector, a friend, a guide into our world. You only need to ask. Trust is earned—I understand that—I only want the chance to earn yours."

My heart stumbles and a weird sense of belonging threatens to take me over. The truth of his conviction rings in his words and a shiver of pleasure races down my spine. But I know the truth about belonging. When it's taken away, your emotions are stripped bare and you're left all alone.

Kotah's likely too young to be jaded by the harshness of reality. He isn't naïve exactly, but he also isn't a typical twenty-year-old. Judging by his response to me asking his age, I'd bet he tires of being sized up by his outer package.

"May I ask you something odd—and feel free to say no."

He flashes me a sheepish grin. "What is it?"

Now I feel silly. My life is spiraling out of control and my libido keeps grabbing the reins. "I'm dying to touch your hair. Would you mind?"

Kotah laughs and shifts sideways on the seat. His movements stretch his side, his shirt rucking up to expose perfectly sculpted abs and muscled hips. "Of course, you can."

Even with him relaxed, I sense the predator within him. He isn't alpha like the jaguar and the hawk, or a beta like the bear, but he still defended me with his life last night.

He unties the leather string at the tail of his braid and runs his fingers through the plaits to set the lengths free. Then, he stretches his arm across the back of the seat of the truck and leans closer. His hair hangs like a silky, chestnut drape, the ends reaching down to the seat.

His handsome face, so open and guileless unlocks something inside me. I found him disarming yesterday.

Today, it's more.

"I'm sorry you suffer, Calli," he whispers. "If it were within my powers, I would bear the turmoil for you and ease your transition." He brushes the back of my hand and another rush of emotional calm takes me over.

Oh… *he's* doing that.

Warning flares within me at the thought of my emotions being manipulated—but no. Connected as we are, I sense his intentions. He is only caring for my wellbeing.

I swallow and a deep longing triggers inside me.

My dominant instinct is to claim what's mine. I imagine crawling over his hips and straddling him. He'd let me. He possesses completely different energy than the others—shyness and excitement versus male dominance and swagger.

Kotah is sweetness and support swirling around in an intelligent, principled, clean-cut, genuine guy.

"How can I sense your aggression level in the hierarchy of things? You aren't standoffish like the others. You don't feel the need to push in and take over."

"I'm an omega," he says. "In the hierarchy of wildling personalities, there are alphas, betas, submissives, and, on rare occasions, omegas."

"How rare?" I ask, seeing the most adorable blush pinking up his cheeks.

"About one in eight-hundred and forty-three."

"About." I laugh.

Kotah blinks at me like he doesn't understand why I find his answer funny. "You're right, though," he says. "I don't need to dominate you. My sole desire is to help you adjust and ensure your well-being."

Omega. I make a mental note to learn more about that later. If he and I are both so rare, how did we end up together in this? Is that part of the universe's master plan or a happy fluke? Another mystery about my wolf.

Kotah cants his head to the side again, dangling his hair toward me. He reminds me so much of a curious puppy that I almost giggle. Instead, I accept what he offers.

Unlike when I chickened out yesterday with Jaxx, I brush gentle fingers across the prominent bone structure of Kotah's cheek. The sensation of physical contact is both exciting and grounding. It's as if I sense our energy mingling. The connection tingles and travels from the pads of my fingers, up to my wrist, into my body, and straight to my racing heart.

Kotah sits very still, and I continue my exploration into the silky length of his hair. It's as soft as I imagined. I bring my other hand up and rake my fingers past both his temples and back. My eyes roll back as my instincts burst to life. I know—without doubt—my wolf will never hurt me.

"Why are things so much clearer today?"

Kotah swallows and draws a deep breath. "You completed your first shift. Wildling power and intuition grows stronger with each connection we make with our animal selves. Our senses extend beyond what humans comprehend: instincts, pheromones, body language, scents in the air. It's a chaotic muddle of stimuli at first, but in time, your instincts and abilities will be as strong in your human form as they are when you're lighting up."

Lighting up. Flaming out. My life is sure different.

Heat ignites in my chest as I focus on the memory of the trucker and what happened at the side of the road. Without meaning to, I reconnect to the powerful fury of my phoenix taking its revenge on Plaid Nightmare.

"I killed that trucker."

"From what we saw, he deserved it."

I won't argue. My reaction isn't remorse or guilt, it's about the lack of it. What I feel is pure, primal satisfaction. "What kind of animal does it make me that I'm glad?"

Kotah grins. "The kind that survives. You're no longer solely human, Calli. You are a wildling and with that comes the duality of having a creature of instinct inside you. Everything about your human self will be heightened. It's a very exciting time for you."

A twinge of longing shoots through me. Brant, Nakotah, and Hawk saw what I did, my rage, my violent disregard for that trucker's life. They must also know what I did to—

"Jaxx. How is he?"

Kotah's smile falters and my heart sinks. "Not well, I'm afraid. Jaxx can't hold either form or heal as he should. Brant's doctor friend is tending to him, but there is severe damage. We don't know how long he'll be able to continue."

*Oh, gawd. I did that.*

I need to go to him. I close my eyes and focus on the pull of longing tugging at my soul. I need to comfort him. To make it right.

I blink as Kotah squeezes my hand and pulls it off the handle of the door. His easy gaze is gone, replaced by puzzlement. "Are you all right, Calli?"

"Yeah, sorry. I, uh… I was thinking about how badly I need to go to Jaxx."

Kotah kisses the knuckles of my hand and winks. "If

you've changed your mind and wish to go now—"

"No. I need to finish Sonny and help those girls. I owe that to Riley."

"In either case, there's no need to vault from a moving vehicle. You've had enough roadside trauma for one week."

Was I really about to—yeah, I think I was.

I swallow, shaken by how overpowering these instincts are growing. Kotah is still leaning close, looking worried.

He's so freaking adorable.

*Carpe the diem, girlfriend.* Riley says in my head.

There's no stopping the impulse. I close the distance and seal our first kiss. I mean it to be a fast and flirty brush of mouths, to thank him for his kindness and support. Except, the moment our lips touch my animal side explodes. In a thundering rush of ache, I revisit my impulse of five minutes ago and straddle him on the back seat.

Heat hits from everywhere at once, inside and out.

The leather of the seat creaks as Kotah leans back and strong hands press against the blanket on my back. Annoyed with the barrier between his touch and my body, I reach around and drop the blanket to the side.

The breeze coming in from the window caresses my heated skin and I remember that I'm naked. I freeze.

"What is it?" Kotah says, breathless.

Embarrassment burns my cheeks as I look down at how I'm straddled, naked over a young guy I barely know. "Sorry. I didn't mean to mount you like a horny teenager."

Kotah chuckles and his tension eases. "Don't apologize on my account. Wildlings don't have the same hang-ups as humans. Sex is embraced and our sense of modesty is lost during puberty while we learn to control our shifts. I was naked most of the time between the ages of ten and fourteen. It's a reality of our world."

The picture in my mind makes me giggle. I imagine Kotah and his peers flashing from wolf to child at inopportune moments and ending up naked at school and during holiday celebrations. "Hopefully you grew up somewhere warm."

Kotah shakes his head. "I'm a northern boy. Lots of snow and frost to nip at my male parts during the winter."

I glance down at his male parts. There's a beautiful mound pressing against the front of his jeans and I wish I had the magical ability to flash away clothes as they do.

"What are you thinking?" Kotah asks, his voice unsteady. He swallows hard and I watch as his throat bobs behind the wide leather choker he wears. "Whatever it is, my answer is yes. Anything you want."

Gawd, this one melts me. I lower my lips and resume our kiss. It's not as frantic as a moment ago, but it soon builds in momentum. He's addictive.

Kotah grips my hips, urging me forward and gawd it feels so good to have his hands on my skin. I push my breasts against his chest and the fabric of his shirt toys with my nipples. The friction of peaked tips against the cotton is powerful, energizing, so damned arousing.

"Fuck me," Brant says from the front seat. "That's what I'm talking about."

A week ago, I would've been horrified at such a brazen display, but right now, all I want is to open the fly of Kotah's jeans and lap dance him until we both scream out.

I know he's young and inexperienced, but damn, this boy can kiss. His tongue meets mine, stroke for stroke as he grips my hair and splays a firm hand against my spine. I groan as he shifts me over the swell in his jeans. His erection juts hard against the denim. I swear he's about to split the seams.

His hunger drives my need even higher.

*Gawd.* How can this much desire not consume me?

My hips circle. My clit finds the ridge of his cock and then an auspiciously placed seam. So good. I'm lost in the wild of whatever spell I'm under and embrace the pleasure.

There is no anger or loss here with him. There is no destiny calling. There's nothing but Kotah and me.

His cock.

My pussy.

His hands.

My nipples.

Kotah sucks my bottom lip into his mouth. He growls, and his chest vibrates between us. He nips the tender flesh of my mouth, harder than a love bite, but not enough to draw blood. It's a sultry pleasure with just a hint of pain.

Anticipation builds in a hot pang between my legs. I had no idea kissing could feel like this. He's fire. And I long to be burned. Power surges through my body—a power I've never felt before.

I grip the back of the seat, flip my head back, and grind my clit over the ridge of Nakotah's cock, gasping. My need tightens viciously, then releases in a fiery burst of pleasure.

My orgasm pours through me in a scorching wave. I cry out, lost to the primal connection between us. I writhe, riding out a shattering release. It momentarily obliterates my defenses. I want this. I need it. I need so much more of this.

I catch my breath and claim his mouth once more. I can't get enough of his kiss and his outdoorsy scent of earth and wilderness. I grip the back of the seat as sensation ebbs through me in powerful waves. I'm panting, my insides throbbing. I go for his fly. "I want you out of these jeans and inside me, *now*."

"Hey, beautiful," Brant says softly behind me. "I *hate* to interrupt the show, but the truck seat is on fire.

"What? Oh, shit." I let go of the leather seat behind Kotah's head and twist to grab the fire blanket. 'On fire' is a bit of an overstatement but smoldering and melting under my heated touch is just as embarrassing. "Damn it."

Kotah takes over with smothering the fledgling fire and I sink onto the seat.

Brant offers an apologetic smile. "Yeah, even with the fire taken care of, Hawk is back. Devouring the kid will have to wait if you want the drow vendetta as your priority. I'm so fucking sorry, you two."

I whimper at the thought of not having my wolf's cock inside me. Wait. Hawk's back? I rein in my wanton and lift my head to look out the back window. We're parked off in the trees at a rest stop and Hawk is leaning against a light standard a couple of empty spots away.

"When did we get here?"

The deep rumble of Brant's laughter brings me back to my senses. "Not sure. I woke up about fifteen minutes ago and he was already gone."

What? Here I am, totally macking on my wolf, right in front of two other guys, and I'm so lost in lust I missed Hawk parking the truck and heading out to gather intel?

Well, yeah. I also missed setting the truck on fire.

I lean back and press my fingers to my lips, trying to corral the carnal need that possesses me. I eye the damp, creamed mess in Kotah's lap and realize that is the result of me grinding on him. "I, uh… sorry about that."

Brant waves away my embarrassment. "Don't apologize. It's going to get away on us from time to time and I certainly didn't mind. It doesn't look like Kotah is suffering terribly much either, eh kid?"

Kotah rubs strong hands down both my arms and smiles. Thankfully, he's as shaken and breathless as me. "No suffering here. That was incredible."

I swallow. "What I meant to give you was a simple, thank you kiss, for your kindness and support." This time I kiss him on the cheek and keep my hands behind my back. The position makes my chest stick out and his gaze drops to the peaked tips of my nipples.

"You're welcome," Kotah says, his voice strained. "If you don't mind Brant keeping you company for a moment, I need to duck inside the rest station for a moment."

Kotah opens the truck door and bails out.

His hasty departure spikes a wave of concern. I grab the fire blanket, pull it around my shoulders, and step out into the late morning air.

Padding barefoot with Brant over to where Hawk is drawing on a cigarette, I watch Kotah disappear into the men's side of the rest station. "Did I upset him? Should I go check on him?"

Brant chuckles and Hawk's stoic scowl breaks for the first time. It's weird to see the unfamiliar curve of a smile on his lips.

"What?" I say, my frustration bouncing between the two of them. "What am I missing?"

Hawk exhales an expensive smelling tobacco and tugs the ends of his vest down. The hint of his smile is gone as quickly as it has appeared. Honestly, it didn't suit him as much as his rough, broody disposition. "There's nothing wrong with the boy that five minutes alone with his right hand won't ease. Better he let the pressure off here and now than go into a battle with blue balls and a fractured attention span."

*Oh.* Heat warms my cheeks.

Suddenly, I want to chase after him and watch. But gross, I don't want our first sexual encounter to be in the stall of a rest stop. Actually, I guess it was in the back seat of Hawk's Navigator. *Really?* Back seat of a car? Am I sixteen?

"What the hell is wrong with me?" I say, raking my fingers through my hair. "I've never been an exhibitionist and yet I almost ripped off Kotah's jeans to ravish him. I want to race back to be with Jaxx. I want to climb you like a jungle gym plaything," I say, gesturing to Brant. Then I look to Hawk. "And so help me, I want to test how dominant you are when we're both naked and tethered up."

That outburst earns me an encouraging nod from Brant and one hell of a wicked flash of emotion from Hawk. A shiver races through me as if his gaze is visceral, brushing over my heated flesh, and turning up the dial of my pumping heart. My mind is shocked, but my body isn't.

"Careful what you wish for, Spitfire," Hawk says. "That kind of thinking is liable to get you into trouble."

My nipples harden at the thought. "Challenge accepted."

Hawk arches a dark brow. "You couldn't handle it."

But I want to. *Gawd I want to.* My mind spins with all kinds of ideas.

Hawk frowns and his muscles tighten. His shoulders and biceps visibly grow more rigid as he stalks closer.

It's the hottest thing I've ever seen.

"Do you want to avenge your friend or fuck?" he asks, driving his cigarette into the butt-out sand he's standing next to. The full focus of Hawk's attention steals the breath from my lungs. "The two options are not mutually exclusive, mind, but one seems more time-sensitive than the other. Your quest. Your friend. Your choice."

Right. Riley. I owe it to her to stay focused.

# CHAPTER EIGHT

*Calli*

Facing the trees, I flap the blanket wrapped around my shoulders and shiver as my skin cools. "I swear I'm heating up again."

"You likely are." Brant's gaze narrows on the shadows of the woods opposite where we've parked. I bet if anyone happens to be in the trees taking their dog for a pee, he'll race over and poke their eyes out with his claws.

"I need to learn how you guys materialize clothes."

"No," Hawk says flatly. "You need to learn how to control the fire of your phoenix. Clothes won't help if your skin is molten hot."

Well, yeah, there's that.

Kotah jogs back to our dysfunctional meeting of the minds and the guys give him a bro-nod to welcome him back to the fold. "Hawk, what did you learn?"

Hawk turns a cool smile to me. "The most interesting thing is that our Spitfire is curious about kink. Less interesting, is that the drow MC had a barn filled with enough weapons to take out three states and a locked freight box being guarded by men with automatic weapons."

"That must be where the women are," I say.

"Wait," Brant says. "You said *had.* Why the past tense."

"Two FCO teams moved in five minutes ago and seized the site."

"*What?*" I shout. "Without me? We had a deal."

Hawk scowls. "We had no deal. You lied that you'd stay out of it. I made it clear you wouldn't be put in harm's way."

"I'm not nearly as helpless as you think."

"And not nearly as equipped to handle an onslaught of magical attack as *you* think."

Fire sparks off my fingers and I don't even care. Let him get burned. Let it draw the attention of people. If he's so hellbent on handling everything, let him clean up all the messes I make. I curl my fingers into fists and move directly before him. "You had no right to do that without me. I need to set things right for Riley."

He smacks at his shirt when a spark takes hold and starts melting a hole in the fabric. "Yeah, I noted your commitment to the task while you were busy masturbating on the kid. It's over now. Done deal."

"So, you got Sonny?"

Hawk's gaze narrows. "What you fail to realize, Spitfire, is that this is bigger than you and your friend. The illegal activity of these men was brought to my attention before any of this phoenix mess ever exploded in our face. If your friend brought the human police into it, that's a bad thing for us. Let the FCO handle it from here."

"You already knew about the Black Knight before Calli told you?" Brant asks, his attention focused.

I wasn't about to be sidetracked. "Sonny? Did you get him? Will he pay?"

Hawk curses. "You're a pit-bull on a pant leg."

"Glad you're getting that. So, what about Sonny?"

The storm brewing in Hawk's cold, gray eyes gives me my answer before he does. "He's not in custody, but we'll get him. And before you say anything, there was nothing you could've done differently to bring him down. The women won't be sold and defiled. The guns are out of their hands. You ensured your friend's sacrifice meant something."

I can't breathe. I'm so angry at him, at myself, at the world… I should've been there. "You took this from me, Hawk, and I'll never forgive you for that."

"Aw… my heart is broken. The mean man made an executive decision to keep you alive. Poor little girl."

"Stop talking to me like I'm a child."

"Stop acting like one and I'll consider it."

"You're such an arrogant ass."

"Glad you're getting that."

The two of us glare at one another, breathing heavily. I hate him. Yet, every part of me is so alive right now I'm not sure if I attack him if I'll rip him to shreds or rip his clothes off. Damn, this mating heat is seriously annoying.

"What now?" Kotah asks.

Hawk gestures to the tour bus pulling into the rest

station. The long, black and gold vehicle passes the first driveway that joins the cars parked in front and steers behind the building to wrap around to us, stopping in one of the long, bus and transport spots.

When the air brakes squelch, the door to the bus opens and the driver steps out. Hawk points to the square-jawed, ebony-haired man sporting a double shoulder harness. The way he carries himself and surveys his surroundings, he exudes military training. I'd bet he's locked and loaded at all times. "Everyone, this is Lukas. He brought the jaguar and Brant's doctor friend to meet us. Since Calli refused to return to the safehouse, I thought this the next best thing."

My mind spins and I look at the bus. It's the kind of decked-out vehicle that rock bands use while on nation-wide tours. "What? Wait. Jaxx is in there?"

Hawk nods. "Unlike your dead friend, Jaxx actually needs your help."

"Is he all right?"

Hawk rolls his eyes. "Far from it. According to Brant's friend, his system won't take much more of this situation. Doc believes you're the only one who can save him now."

I balk at that. Me?

"Of course." Kotah's eyes sparkle with understanding. "Yes, that's an inspired idea. You can do this, Calli."

Whatever damage I caused by clubbing Jaxx in the head is killing him and that fact is killing me. I've never been one to stick around and take responsibility for my reckless decision-making but here I am.

Look at me—adulting.

"How?" I ask, looking from Hawk to Kotah for a clue. "I don't know anything about fixing people."

"No," Hawk snaps. "Only how to break them."

I give the asshole a middle-fingered salute as he climbs the curved steps of the bus and heads inside.

"Ignore him, beautiful," Brant says, close to my ear. "Focus on what's important. Jaxx needs you."

I follow behind the burly frame of my bear as we pass through the living area and past a kitchenette to the back bedroom at the end of the hotel on wheels. I watch the broad span of his back as he walks, marveling at the clench and release of muscles. He's a big boy but is also cut and carved like a sculpted god.

When we arrive at the back of the bus, he stops. Filling the frame of the bedroom doorway, he turns to me looking grim. "It's not good. There might be nothing anybody can do even if you do try. Keep that in mind, yeah?"

I swallow hard and draw a deep breath. "Kotah thinks I can help. I want to try."

After hesitating a moment longer, Brant opens the way and walks me inside. The room is dark except for whatever industrious rays of light are fighting through the crack of the closed blinds.

Jaxx groans and flashes from man to cat. It's not the magical shift like when he shifted in the garden and introduced himself yesterday. This transformation is violent and jerky and looks terribly painful. It seems like he's stuck mid-shift and getting electrocuted because his body is out of phase.

I press a hand to my chest. "I'm so sorry, Jaxx."

"Prove it," Another man says, staring up at me from Jaxx's bedside. He's got the same build as Brant, but smaller and with dark hair and eyes. "You're the only one who can save him, now."

"I still don't understand."

Kotah shifts closer and runs a gentle hand over my shoulder. "Remember what I said about how powerful a phoenix's healing ability is?"

"Yes, but how do I—a blood transfusion?" I stick my arm out from the fire blanket ready to roll on that.

Kotah shakes his head. "No, not blood. Phoenix *tears* are said to be the strongest medical miracle in existence. There are tales in the lore of incredible feats of healing from a few shed tears absorbed. It's plain in your face that you regret what happened. I think what Doc is suggesting is for you to feel that and shed tears for him."

My breath locks frozen in my chest.

*Shit.* "I want to help. I… uh, but I'm not much of a tear-jerker girl."

Brant frowns down at me. "Try Calli. Sit with him and let it sink in. He needs your help. You gotta try."

I shuffle across the floor even though I don't know what good it will do. I haven't cried in over twelve years—not since my parents' funeral. Not since everything I loved about life was torn away.

"Hey, Jaxx," I say, struggling with the length of the fire blanket as I crawl onto the bed. It catches under my knee and after a few awkward tugs, I lay beside the gorgeous golden jaguar. The spotted cat lifts his boxy head and I think a flash of recognition hits. I wait for betrayal to darken those stunning turquoise eyes, but it doesn't come.

Instead, there is only tenderness and relief.

"Jaxx is worried about you," Doc says, standing at the edge of the bed behind me. "Every moment he's lucid, he fights with me to go find you. He's a good man, dedicated to your safety and your bond as mates."

I don't miss the censure in his voice and glance over my shoulder to match his hostile glare. "Thank you for taking care of Jaxx, but you don't know me, Bear. You're not part of this mess and you don't get an opinion."

He offers me a sad smile. "Maybe not, but Brant is my friend and he deserves better than a club to the back of the skull. Should I stick close in case you try to take another one of your guardians out?"

Heat explodes in the center of my chest as fiery rage claws to get out. "Careful. I'm not in control of my fire yet and picking at me makes me want to flame out and torch you to a crisp."

Brant moves in fast and steps between us. "But you won't. We need Doc to help Jaxx. Besides, you don't actually want to hurt him."

I give Doc what I hope is a convincing smile. "Yes. I do. You don't know me well yet either, big guy, but I'll never be voted Miss Congeniality."

Brant's expression seems frozen between surprise and sexual turn-on. It's a look I'm getting used to the more time I spend with him. He turns to his buddy and gestures to the door. "Maybe some distance would be good, Doc. Calli needs to focus on Jaxx."

Doc eases back, his gaze locked on me. "I get that your animal side is powerful and protective. So, too, is my loyalty. You'd do well to remember that."

Brant grumbles something as he clears his friend from the room, and I uncurl my fingers from white-knuckled fists.

I look at Hawk and Brant standing at the bedside behind me, and then Kotah on the other side of Jaxx. I close my eyes and draw a steadying breath. "I don't care what he thinks, but you three need to understand how sorry I am. I was scared and confused. I wanted to get away. I've never had the strength to hurt a man before. I made a terrible but honest mistake."

Hawk laughs and waves away my apology. "Please. You may never have possessed wildling strength before, but you've left a path of destruction in your wake your whole, pathetic life."

A deep-chested rumble fills the air as Brant straightens to his full height. "Avian, if you don't want to be here, then fuck off. We don't need a pompous dick as part of our bonding. If we promise to miss you, will you go away?"

Hawk steps toward the end of the bed, his steel-gray gaze swinging toward Brant. "Are you so pussy-whipped that you buy into her performance?"

Kotah huffs and adjusts the frame of his glasses. "Avians may be a solitary race, but that doesn't excuse the way you speak to people, Hawk. Whatever your issue is, it's wrong for you to take it out on us."

"Not you, kid. *Her.*" Hawk's voice drips with disdain. "Our little mate is a white trash liar and you three don't see it. Do you honestly think she'll bow over poor Jaxx and weep tears of remorse? Please, she doesn't have it in her."

Hawk's words hit too close to home. He isn't wrong. The others look at me and see the potential of what they believe I can be. Hawk is shrewder.

Brant scowls. "How about you give her a minute to adjust before you point fingers and write her off? It's been a crazy couple of days."

"I *do* feel horrible about what happened," I say.

Hawk stalks closer. The tension in his muscles gives off palpable energy that makes the hair on my arms stand on end. He grips the end of the bed and leans forward. "You may regret Jaxx's brain damage but way down deep you're doing a fucking jig. You've got a real-life Cinderella story unfolding here, don't you?"

I bark a laugh. "How do you figure?"

He stretches his hands out as if clearing the stage for a grand tale. "Calliope Tannis, the sad, orphan child is shipped off to live with an aunt who doesn't want her half as much as the skeevy husband does. How old were you when you realized you couldn't stay, Calli? Thirteen? Fourteen? You saw the writing on the wall and knew she'd pick him over you."

I freeze, reading his eyes. His words ripple through my body, triggering a violent tide of anger and revulsion. My body explodes with the fury of what happened and what could have happened if I stayed. "I was a kid. My aunt was supposed to protect me—"

"But she chose her husband over blood family. So, robbing her blind was fair game, right? Take what you need and look out for number one at all costs. No one here blames you for seeking a bit of security in life."

*Seeking security.* "Because of them, I had to live on the streets. There was no security." My heart pounds, banging to get free of my ribs.

"So, who can blame you for what you turned into?"

"Shut up," I snap, my mind spinning. "That wasn't my fault. You don't know anything about me. You don't know what happened or how hard I fought to survive."

Hawk laughs. "I know every detail, Calli. I had a file on you the same day the bond locked into place. Did you think I'd simply accept you as an equal? I have an image to protect, a corporate brand I represent. I get ahead of publicity nightmares by knowing who I'm in bed with. I know all your dirty little secrets."

He's not bluffing. My lockbox of past humiliations blows wide open and my skin crawls. It's taken years of guilt and self-destruction to bury my past and Hawk digs it up with a smile and throws it in my face?

"I survived to tell the tale."

He casts me a cold smile. "You did. You spent the next decade with Riley lying, stealing, and begging for scraps. Are you culpable for any of that? Is any of that your fault?"

"You weren't there."

"But I was—that's the point. I transformed myself from a penniless runaway, to start my own company and take over the world. I did it with my head held high and without compromising my ethics. Look how high I rose taking the high road. Women throw themselves at me, Calli, beautiful women of breeding and education. They've got class and style and I devour them like ambrosia. Now I'm supposed to be ball-and-chained to a two-bit lying hustler for the rest of my life?"

He passes a withering gaze over me and frowns.

Piercing pain impales my heart and my phoenix shrieks inside me. The mating bond tilted my world on its axis, but he wants other women?

"Yeah, you're the shit," I say, my eyes stinging.

A cruel smile curves his lips. "Until four days ago, I was. Now, according to shifter legend, my cock will never rise for another and everything I built now belongs to you, my queen. You are the be-all-end-all to our lives—you—a scared little girl who never earned anything except a reputation on the streets and an underage rap sheet."

I catch the horror in Nakotah's gaze and his face blurs behind a wall of moisture.

Brant prowls to the end of the bed. "Shut your fucking mouth and get out. That's enough."

Hawk chuffs and holds his ground. "So, she gets four beck and call boys and you're not pissed at the tradeoff? I lose my life's work, the jaguar gets brain damage, the kid loses out on his dream of becoming a scholar, and you haven't realized it yet, but your sex life just got a whole lot less interesting. She's the only one of us sitting in the winner's circle here."

Brant swings. Hawk evades. He's smaller but fast. Brant takes another run at him and they slam into the bedroom wall. The bus rocks as the sound of fists to flesh fill the room.

"Stop!" I shout. "Both of you, now."

The fury rippling off the two of them as they face

off feels all wrong. It hurts my insides. Instinct tells me that I'm supposed to be the core of the bond.

Instead, I'm the conflict.

I swipe at the moisture dripping off my chin and pull a labored breath into tight lungs. "Brant, please stop. Please."

He lets off an ear-shattering roar and stumbles back.

Hawk straightens, glances over at me, and looks as smug as ever.

I swallow against the lump in my throat. "You may think you have me figured out, but you're not as smart as you think you are."

Hawk steps away from my bear and laughs. "Please, I've bathed in women like you. You're nothing special Calli. We all know it. Our world needs greatness right now. Hard truth time—that isn't you. Do you honestly think you can step up and claim the reins to protect a species of people you know nothing about?"

No. I don't.

"I didn't think so. You haven't got it in you."

Brant growls. "Not. Another. Word. That's *enough*."

Hawk holds up his palms. "Agreed—it's more than enough. It's too much. When Jaxx dies, we go to the Bastion as planned and have the Elder Council sever us from this magical mistake as we talked about. If a phoenix is needed, we'll find a better one than her."

Tears stream down my cheeks as fire burns the back of my throat. They planned to sever our bond. They think I'm a mistake. The wildness inside me reels to break free. Damn it. Yesterday I fought to deny our bond, now it physically hurts to think of it being taken from me.

When did I buy into the idea that I could be more? That I could belong to something amazing? I grip the blanket to quell my shaking hands. The threat of breaking the bond of my mates hurts at a depth of emotion I don't understand.

I can't bear to meet the gaze of Kotah or Brant. Squeezing my eyes shut, I curl around Jaxx and cry.

I wish I died in that stupid ditch.

# CHAPTER NINE

*Hawk*

Fuck me. I've flayed people to the bone in the pursuit of something I want in business a thousand times but ripping Calli to shreds isn't that. The cruelty that leveled her gave me no pleasure. The betrayal and horror in her eyes pierced me to the same damaged part of my own blackened soul. The only truth I spoke was that I *do* know her—I fucking *am* her.

I see the walls erected around her emotions and knew she'd never be able to cry to heal Jaxx—not without help.

Reading people is my fucking superpower. I can follow the tension in someone's furtive glance and instinctively drill into their most private pain. That skill coupled with what my team dug up on Calli made reducing her to shattered shards too easy.

Yeah, so who's the one who's really broken?

Life smashed me into so many pieces at a young age that I'll never be Humpty Dumptied enough to belong in this mating quint. The odd man out is nothing new.

Hated and envied is my wheelhouse.

Heavy footsteps gain on me as I drop out of the bus and head for the rest station. Of course, Brant needs to play the part of Calli's big bad protector. It's in his genetic makeup.

Rough hands grab my shoulder and whip me around. I don't resist. His fist connects with my face and knocks me back in an explosion of black spots in my vision. His grip tears the front of my custom-fitted shirt as a rush of blood sprays from my mouth and nose.

The pain soothes my aching soul like a masochistic balm. I deserve this. Fuck. The bear has fists like concrete.

But yeah, I deserve this.

Huffing like it's an effort not to rip me to shreds, Brant pushes his broad chest at me. "You're a steaming piece of shit, Hawk. A real piece of work."

"You're welcome."

Brant stares like he knocked my block loose and I'm not tracking. Nope. I recognized what needed to be done and did it. Calli wasn't about to unleash tearful regret over Jaxx and our golden boy didn't have time for them to figure that out.

"You shattered our girl. For what?"

To keep the quint whole.

He'll never believe that. I test my jaw and push at a few teeth. I pull myself upright and check that my legs still work. If Jaxx died, Calli would never forgive herself and she'd never grow into the phoenix our people need. "Big picture, Bear. The five of us need to up our game for what's to come."

"You alienated her—humiliated her. She'll never

forgive what you said or how you said it."

Brant's words drive another stake into my cold, dark heart. I hold my expression tight and head to the closest toilet to be sick.

"You're an asshole," the bear shouts at my back.

"You're welcome."

When I finish in the washroom, I pat my mouth with a length of gritty paper towel and pop a mint. I find Lukas outside the bus doors. The man's been with me the better part of a decade. I trust his skills as much as his loyalty. "Their life and well-being are now linked to your own. Consider yourself warned."

"Of course, Mr. Barron," he says, accustomed to the truth behind my threat. "We'll await your return unless directed otherwise."

"And the other thing I asked about?"

Lukas hands me a stack of loaded magazines and I nod. "Spelled to take down drow?"

Lukas dips his chin. "As requested."

"And Jayne? Is she handling the scheduling for the Monster Rights conclave?"

"For now. The meeting is still set for next week. She wanted me to remind you to check in before that or risk losing the good will you've earned."

Yeah, no. Despite the unknown status of my personal life, I won't let Calli derail my business goals. "Understood."

That taken care of, I pop the back hatch of my truck and key in my lock code to open the safe built into the luggage compartment floor. With military precision, I strap on a flack vest, slide two of the magazines Lukas prepared for me into the ammo pockets and eject the magazines from my twin Sig forties. Once my usual hollow point performance rounds are replaced with the drow ammo in my guns, I holster them and rub a shammy over the camera lens on my sternum.

"Prefer to battle like a human, do you?" Brant asks the insult clear in his timbre. "Can't cut it as a Hawk?"

I shut the hatch and smile through the insult. Prejudice against avians is real. All the big, burly species of wildlings think that their teeth and muscles take them to the top of the predator list. They underestimate cunning and stealth. "A man like me garners enemies, both nary and not. You know the saying, 'Always be prepared.'"

Brant chuffs. "Except you're no Boy Scout."

I bare my teeth. "And don't forget it."

When I slide behind the wheel, I'm struck by the acrid stench of charred leather and the feminine scent of Calli's orgasm. The bastardized scent hangs fragrantly in the air of the cab. Fuck me. Another wave of self-hatred swamps me.

I lower the windows and lock my reaction away with the rest of my loathing. "Get in, Bear. You're no use to anyone here. You might as well come help with the clean-up."

The guy glances back at the bus. "I should stay with Calli. She's upset."

I roll my eyes. "Lukas, Doc, and the kid can babysit Calli. Last I checked, you work for me. How about you show me what you can do in the field."

Brant opens the passenger's door, clicks his seatbelt,

and glares over at me. "I'm an FCO Enforcer and a damned good one. Don't think for a second that I work for you. I work for the fae community and I'll take down anyone who's fucking with the system for their own purposes."

"Uh-huh. Is that supposed to mean something to me?"

"Hard to know if anything means something to you."

I adjust the rear-view and see Calli's melted handprints in the leather. Is this my life now, bumping into one reminder after the next of how the universe fucked me over?

Hard pass.

I cast a sideways glance and catch the disapproving scowl locked on Brant's face. I turn the key and the beefy engine rumbles to life. "Oh, for shit's sake. Yes, I'm a mean man. I hurt your girlfriend's feelings. Head in the game, Bear. You didn't want her at that property any more than I did."

Christ. One day into this disaster and they've all lost their damned minds. It's maddening. What kind of male allows his world to get overturned by sad eyes and killer curves?

I curse myself. Yeah, fuck off.

One look at Calli, one breath of her scent in my lungs, one feminine note of her voice in my ears, and I fell victim to the same fate. I'm as pathetic as the others.

And I *hate* it.

"The property we're heading for has a chinked-log bungalow, a large barn, and a secured, underground bunker in the woods out back. What I didn't say in front of Calli is that all the women in the freight container were already dead."

"You lied to her. You said they were free."

"No. I said they were recovered and wouldn't be defiled and sold to monsters."

"Semantics. You misled her."

I merge onto the highway and check my rear-view. "She's suffering from the loss of her friend. Her friend died to save those women. What do you think it will do to her to know that her efforts ended with little success? While she lay in a comfy bed sleeping for three days after her transition, eighteen women died, trapped in a steel tomb. She knew they were there and instead of telling someone who could help, she opted for revenge and they all died."

"You can't seriously blame her."

"I don't, but trust me, Bear—she will."

Thankfully, my shotgun seat falls quiet and I'm left to my thoughts for the rest of the drive. What Kotah is to IQ, Brant is to heart. The guy feels things to the marrow of his oversized bones. Part of me envies that kind of compassion.

A bigger part of me doesn't.

What use would I be if I caught a case of the feels?

As my mind drifts, I catch sight of the back seat and revisit the sexual scene I was privy to an hour ago. As much as it pisses me off, I'm not nearly as immune to our sexy little mate as I want to be.

When she was grinding on the cub, my cock was so hard and demanding I had to park and bail. Even from thirty feet away and with my attention firmly scanning the rest stop, instead of the interior of my truck, Calli's orgasm got to me.

And seriously? The kid is the first one to win the prize?

I let that truth bite me in the ass and glare at the road ahead. How in all that's holy can the universe think that my perfect match is a female drawn to a sweet puppy like him?

Still, she challenged me on kink.

Maybe there's hope for her yet.

The next fifteen minutes are spent in hostile silence, but when we get to the property, it's all business. "I've got an extra vest in the back. I'll introduce you and then leave you to check things out on your own. Let me know if you find anything interesting."

Brant accepts the vest and when he straps it on, he takes an extra moment to flash his big brawny muscles as if that would intimidate me somehow. Not gonna happen.

"I am the Dom, not the Sub. Save the pec winks for someone who cares."

*Jaxx*

I rise in slow, sluggish pulls from the depths of a dark stupor. Despite feeling like I've been run over by a bulldozer, my cells are alive with magic. If my mind wasn't such a muddy fog, I'd track the magical signature and figure out where it's coming from. Instead, I follow the soft sobs of a female to consciousness. No… it's not *a* female, it's *my* female.

Even before I blink awake, I feel Calli curled around my cat form. She's crying like someone ripped her heart in two. Is this about me? I fight to shift back and ease her suffering. I'm not there yet. Whatever happened—

I remember the pain of being struck down in the garden. Were we ambushed? Did someone breach Leo's compound and attack us?

Concern for her gives me the strength to reclaim my human form. I shift and gather her into my arms. The first thing that comes to me is that we're both naked. The second is that she's wrapped in a fire blanket again.

What did I miss?

My arms come around her and she sinks against me. The apprehension and fight that bled from her before are gone. All her soft and curvy melds with my hard and cut.

It's perfection.

The miracle of Calli makes my breath hitch.

She lifts her face and man, yeah, she is a hot mess. My chest isn't faring well either. My skin is soaked, and it dawns on me. The magic I feel is her—phoenix tears.

Calli's power of healing saved my life.

"*Shh*, sweet girl, *shh*. Whatever it is, it's okay—"

"Jaxx," she sobs, my name barely understandable with the breathless gasps and hiccoughs racking her. "I didn't mean to hurt you. I was scared. Hawk's right, I *am* selfish. I'm so sorry you're stuck with me. I understand why you wanted to sever our mating bond. I *am* a mistake."

My mind stumbles, trying to keep up. Sever our bond? Mistake? Wait. Is she saying *she* pole-axed me?

Okay, that stings, but still, I can't stand to see her so

lost. I ease back to see her better. "What's this about?" I bend and kiss the top of her head. Yeah, I missed a lot. She shifted again. The faint trace of char in her scent before, is now much more defined. "I'm all right. S'all good. Tell me what happened."

"None of this is fair to you four. Hawk's right." Calli goes on to tell me about running away, and bikers who killed her best friend, and torching truckers, and a creepy uncle and the aunt who didn't choose her, and everything Hawk put her through about what she did to survive.

When I tighten my hold on her, she sags. "Jaxx, I never meant for any of this to happen. Please, forgive me."

Does she think I won't—that I'll push her away? She doesn't understand mating bonds yet, but I'll show her. "Of course, sweetheart. Forgiven. Forgotten. We're a lock."

After a few more minutes of snuggling, her fall apart ebbs to its end and she pulls herself together like the fighter I know she is.

When I'm sure she's good, I place a gentle finger under her chin and lift her gaze to meet mine. "Ignore Hawk. If I could stand, I'd track the bastard down and gnaw him like a chew toy. As far as I'm concerned, you were reborn on the side of that road. Whatever happened before was your human self. You're a wildling now. You were chosen to be our perfect match and you will be. The past is over and done with. It's the future I'm invested in."

She snuggles tighter against me and I peel back the edge of her blanket to kiss her bare shoulder. "Forget the dirt Hawk slew at you. The only animal that can't fall down is a worm. The rest of us are imperfect. Our life begins now."

Calli rises in my arms and the blanket's coverage falls away. *Hot dayum* she's gorgeous. Sadly, I'm in no condition to show her how amazing I find her.

Right now, we need to heal. "Grab the duvet and cover us up, kitten. I need rest and you need TLC. Let's hunker down for a bit."

When Calli brings up the duvet, I pull the fire blanket around her shoulders and cover her up. "No more tears, sweet girl. Everything will look better when we wake up. I swear."

*Calli*

I wake with a startle when the bus jerks into motion. I blink at the warm, tangerine sunset tinting the tour bus bedroom. I must've dozed off. When I came in to lay with Jaxx, it was mid-afternoon, now it must be nearly dinner time. My heart rate jumps, and I wonder what's next. Will Hawk want to go talk to his council to break our bond? Jaxx doesn't want that. Or Kotah. I'm pretty sure Brant won't want it either, though I haven't had a chance to talk with my bear much yet.

I shift to extract myself from the covers, and Jaxx stirs in his sleep. He tightens the hold of his arm draping over me to keep me close.

Funny. If I woke like this a few weeks ago, I would've panicked. Any man too close when I feel vulnerable triggers my defensive instincts no matter how much I care for him or rationalize. With Jaxx, that cold dread doesn't come.

*He forgives me.*

With an unfamiliar glow warming my chest, I unwrap myself from the blankets and slide out from the comfort of Jaxx's embrace. My jaguar lets off a sexy purr and I'm all smiles as I shuffle into the bathroom.

Set out on the counter of the little vanity area is a white robe made from what feels like the same flame-retardant fabric as my blanket. Sweet.

How weird is it that a bus has a full-sized washroom with shower, toilet, and vanity? Who thought of this? Someone with money to burn.

I think of Hawk and a fresh wave of betrayal hits.

The woman in the mirror catches my attention. With the dust settling from the obliteration of my emotional walls, I see things in a new light. Hawk is wrong. I'm more than my mistakes and the circumstances of a shitty human life. If he wants to sever our bond, he can walk away. He'll be the one making the mistake.

I'll prove to the others I'm more than my past.

I freshen up, shrug on the robe, and pad barefooted past my purring jaguar man sleeping in the bed.

"There she is," Brant says, welcoming me into the lounge to join him and Kotah for what I can only describe as a buffet gone wild. The guys move to stand as I enter the room, and I wave for them to sit back down. "Just in time, beautiful. We figured you and Jaxx would be starving, so we picked up enough food to choke a horse."

I glance at the spread, and the bear isn't exaggerating. There is enough food set out on the counter to feed an army. Well, at least my guardian army. "Where's Hawk?"

Brant tilts his head toward the front of the bus. "He's shot-gunning the way in his truck. Lukas is driving the Navigator while he gets some work done."

"Avoiding me?"

"Avoiding us," Kotah says. "Calli, what he said before… the way he spoke to you…"

I raise a hand and wave away the embarrassment. Nothing Hawk said was untrue, but it doesn't mean I want to dwell on it. "Despite what he thinks, I intend to learn and become the best freaking phoenix your world has ever seen."

Kotah jumps up to kiss my cheek. "And we'll help you. Anything you need."

"Damn skippy," Brant says, handing me a plate and pointing to the food. "We don't need him. If he wants to cut ties, he's welcome to appeal to the elders when we get to the Bastion. The four of us will rock this union and make the fae world proud."

Even the thought of Hawk leaving our bond cleaves me with a piercing loss. I don't know why I care. I'm furious with him. As much as I admire his accomplishments and see how he's an asset to our bonding, I don't like him and I doubt we'll ever be close.

I still don't want him to leave.

My mound of Thai noodles crashes into the stir fry when I plop a scoop of cheesy macaroni and bacon. I throw on a few ribs to round out my food groups and grab a fork. Shuffling to the sectional sofa along the lounge wall, I set my plate down and take a deep breath.

"Since when do I eat like this?"

Brant chuckles. "Since you're fueling a wildling body."

"And do wildlings get fat?"

"Nope."

Well, that's a plus. "Okay, so, what do we do now? Where do we go? I need training and education and likely a lot more that I have no idea I need to know."

Brant turns sideways and slides his leg onto the cushion, to face me. He takes my hand in his and smiles. "We're headed to the Bastion now and will be there sometime before the crack of dawn."

I stiffen and a wave of nausea hits hard. "Why there?"

Brant's nostrils flare and he shakes his head. "It has nothing to do with contesting our bond."

"No, don't think that." Kotah kneels on the floor beside me, places a hand on my thigh, and my anxiety drains away. He smiles and my cells tingle with a rush of warmth and affection. "Don't ever think that."

I swallow. Despite their reassurance now, it guts me they discussed it in the first place. Was it a plan? Did it simply get thrown out as an option? I don't want to know. I'm not strong enough yet to face the rejection. "Okay, then why go there?"

Brant sighs. "As much as it galls me to admit it, Hawk's instinct to go there wasn't all wrong. The Bastion is the central hub for all fae races. He's got more clout behind him than the rest of us combined. We need to find out what triggered your resurrection and why we're meant to open the portal gate? Is it peaceful on the other side or such a war-torn loss that we need to help?"

I grab a napkin to wipe rib juice off my fingers. "I'm not clear on the whole gate thing. If I'm the magical key, how do I open it? Is it a door? Do I just walk up and turn the handle?"

Brant shrugs. "No idea. That's why we need to go to the Bastion. Hawk has clearance to access satellite feeds and security reports. It's our best shot to figure out why we were brought together."

"And," Kotah says. "Once Hawk accesses the satellite feeds, he can track Sonny and his remaining drow forces."

"He's still going to pursue Sonny?"

Brant looks surprised. "Of course. Not only did that drow and his men hurt you, but they are fae rogues killing humans. That's a major offense in our world. Fae live peacefully with humans or we don't live at all. It's our greatest tenet. The Fae Council has to be notified."

Kotah presses a hand on my thigh and releases another round of feel-good mojo.

*The Bastion.* I hate the idea of being near the men who can weigh in on our bond. I also want Sonny and his remaining men to pay for what they've done. I set my plate down and swallow. "Promise me, if you have doubts about being my guardians, you'll come to me first. I hate sounding paranoid, but everyone gets taken from me. I have to know you won't change your mind and leave if things go sideways."

Brant's response is immediate. He scoops me off the couch and sits me in his lap. "Calli, only death could tear me from your side—and maybe not even that."

Kotah presses my hand over his chest. His heart is strong, hammering under my palm. "I am yours for as long as I live or as long as you'll have me."

I draw an unsteady breath.

How can this possibly be my life?

# CHAPTER TEN

*Hawk*

With my laptop open and the secure connection on my cellphone hotspot verified, I finish with my head of operations. “I’m telling you, Hunter, it’s bigger than a few rogues making money illegally. With the number of guns we found in that barn and the ammo in the bunker, there’s an underground force gaining strength.

“Underground force? Mr. Barron, those drow are playing a human corruption game. How can that hold any threat to the fae world? It’s troubling, yes, but likely nothing more than a dark race giving in to a system of greed.”

“What’s really troubling is that we weren’t on top of things and my head of operations isn’t taking the threat seriously. Hunter, if the drow set up this kind of exchange every six months, we need to know how long it’s been going on, who’s on the receiving end of the guns, and where all the money is coming from.”

“Yes, sir. We’ll track it down. I guarantee it.”

“Don’t placate me, Coyote. Just do it. Blind spots are unacceptable, especially with the arrival of a phoenix. I want everything double-checked. There’s a storm brewing. I won't be caught unaware."

I end the call with Hunter and click back to the call in waiting with Jayne. "I'm back."

"I sent the documents. You should have them now."

I open the incoming documents from Jayne.

"You need to take care of this personally, darling," she says, "before your absence and lack of follow-up is perceived as you not giving the Fae Council due consideration."

"If I remember correctly, I set up the Fae Council and helped to create their hierarchy of power. My dedication is well established in the circles of those who matter. Whether I look at land contracts from the top of my office tower or my truck, is no one's business but mine."

"Are you getting enough sleep, darling? You're being unduly terse with me tonight."

I sigh, not really. Flipping from the current land survey to the same map taken from historical record and back again, I frown. "There's a discrepancy on the bottom quadrant of the map in the flow of the river. Why?"

The rustle of paper on the other end of the line indicates that Jayne is referring to the original documents. "It seems the path of the river moved over a century. Natural erosion or flooding likely caused the banks to swell and shift."

"Don't take anything for granted. Have a science team review it and check out the site."

"That's a bit reactive, don't you think? It's likely—"

"Not your call, Miss Trenton. If I'm not mistaken,

*my* likeness hangs in the grand entrance, not yours. You work for me. We are not equals."

"You *are* in a mood," she says. "Very well, I'll arrange a team of surveyors to go out tomorrow. Also, I have several contracts and agreements which require signing. May I at least assume you'll be returning by the week's end?"

"You may not. We ran into trouble with a rogue group of drow. It's taking me to the Bastion. Once that's sorted, I'll reassess things."

"What does that mean?"

"Exactly what I said."

"What has gotten into you this past week? Does it have anything to do with the rumors of a phoenix resurrection? Is there a concealment issue I should be aware of?"

"If your attention was required, I would let you know."

"Why are you being so aloof? I know you too well to believe a personal matter could derail you for an entire week."

I straighten, glaring at the road stretching out before us. It rubs me raw to think people are speculating about the phoenix's arrival. Even worse, I don't want Jayne anywhere near the current Calli bonding mess.

"You worry about the Fae land discrepancy and run things at the office. Courier the documents you need to be signed to Gareth at the Bastion. I'll get them once we arrive."

Without awaiting an answer, I hang up. "Why is it so unbelievable that I might have a personal matter to attend to?"

Lukas grunts. "Other than the fact that you don't permit personal matters in your life?"

"Yes, other than that."

"I'd say that if something came up, you'd handle it with a phone call or a quick verbal response. Flying across the country and spending the next week out of the office is highly out of character."

"I flew to Miami two months ago and stayed a week."

"To oversee the serial murder of a pixie colony. That wasn't personal. You don't do personal. Well, *didn't* before being bound as a Guardian of the Phoenix."

I throw him a scathing look. "You know about that?"

He slides an amused gaze over at me. "I may act the part of your bodyguard and driver but we both know how much more I am than that."

"Well, it's a moot technicality regardless. I'm exploring my options on how to sever the bond. Can you honestly imagine me as a bonded male?"

"Playing well with others has never been your strength."

I chuff and open my next email.

Lukas slows the truck, frowning and I follow his troubled gaze. A person is standing in the middle of the road up ahead, waving us down.

"What's this, now?" Three cars are scattered in a tight cluster across the lanes, blocking quick passage. One man stands alone in front of the blockade waving his arms.

"Stay here, sir. I'll check it out."

*Calli*

The driver's compartment of the tour bus is to the left of the curved stairs that lead outside. From the top step, I lean over to stare out the massive window to see why we stopped. "It looks like a car accident," I holler back to the others. "A guy is in the middle of the road. Lukas is checking it out."

The engine of the bus rumbles beneath my feet as I watch Lukas approach the stranger. He seems apprehensive, searching the barely sprouted farm fields and scattered houses on both sides of the road.

Brant comes up to join the peanut gallery. Before long, he frowns and calls to the back. "Jaxx, do you feel up to taking the wheel for a sec?"

"Yeah, I'm good. Why?"

Brant shrugs. "After years as an enforcer, my Spidey-senses are pretty good. Something about this feels hinky. Doc, you're with me. Let's get those cars moved to the shoulder and get moving again."

A moment later, Jaxx slides into the driver's seat and Kotah swings the handle of the door to seal us in. "Calli? Would you mind stepping back and looking out the window from that seat? I don't like you exposed in front of so much glass."

"Good call," Jaxx says, a thread of tension tight in his voice. With his bare foot on the break, he puts the bus in reverse and grips the steering wheel. "Sitting down is a good idea in case we need to make a quick exit."

The apprehension of the others tightens in my belly.

I'm not sure if it's paranoia or instinct. "Why are we all suddenly on high alert?"

Lukas is twenty feet from the accident now, with Brant and Doc jogging to catch up with him. The guy in the center of the road raises his hand and—

Two sharp *cracks* split the air.

Lukas twists sideways and stumbles behind the bumper of the closest car. He clutches his arm and my heart stops.

Gunshots.

"Fuck," Jaxx says, ramming the gearshift into first. He lets off the brakes and Kotah swings the door open and jumps out of the way.

Hawk runs up the stairs as we jolt backward.

"Wait!" I say, pointing at the scene well out in front of us. "No. We can't leave them!"

I lunge for the steps, but Hawk catches me by the waist and lifts me over his shoulder in a fireman's hold.

"Get us out of here, Jaguar." Hawk's fury rumbles from his chest and vibrates in mine.

Three more shots *crack* off.

The *thunk* of bullets hitting metal rings out against the side of the bus. A window shatters in an explosion of raining glass shards. I protest against Hawk's hold, wriggling and flailing as panic takes root in my gut. "We can't leave. Brant's out there. Lukas is shot."

Hawk doesn't stop until we're in the bedroom. He drops me unceremoniously on the bed and I'm still skidding across the mattress when I'm shielded by a large, snarling wolf.

"You've got guard duty, Wolf," Hawk says, turning from an open safe in the bedside cabinet. "Spitfire, do you know how to handle a gun?"

My mind stumbles. "Point and squeeze?"

Hawk nods. "Point and squeeze works. I'm disengaging the safety, so that's all you'll need to do. But be careful. Kotah is your last line of defense and we don't want the kid bleeding out from friendly fire, all right?"

I swallow and take the gun in my trembling hands. My heart thunders in my chest so hard it feels like my chest might explode. "Who's out there? What do they want?"

The roar of an angry bear outside has me pushing up on my knees and turning for the window behind the bed.

"NO!" Hawk shouts. In the next second, I'm flat on my back with a tightly wound man pressing me into the mattress. "Keep your head down and stay alive. There's no future for any of us if you wind up dead."

I swallow hard. For the first time since I met the unflappable corporate tyrant, I hear a vein of uncertainty in his voice. No, it's not uncertainty—it's fear.

The look he pegs me with is filled with both heated panic and icy disdain. This strange connection we share peels back the emotion and exposes why. He desperately needs me safe, but he wishes he didn't care.

Why *I* care after he flayed me, is as much a mystery, but something primal inside me says it's not the time to take my stand. Counter to my natural SOP, I push down my instinct to fight and succumb—for the moment—to the needs of the man who only hours ago reduced me to shreds.

That emotional resonance must flow both ways because his ego deflates. He releases my wrists and straightens beside the bed. "Keep your head down. I'll help the others."

I nod and sink my fingers deep into the warm coat of my wolf. Hawk never answered my question about what the gunmen want, but he doesn't have to.

It's written in the fury on his face.

*Me.* If Brant and the others die out there, it's because they are protecting me.

Hawk's gone in another heartbeat and I hug Kotah. "I hate that this is happening. I don't even understand—"

An ear-shattering explosion *cracks* behind me.

Glass rains down on me in thick chunks. I lunge forward as something grabs my robe at the nape of my neck. I'm yanked backward, up and over the window frame, and fall twenty feet to the asphalt.

My hip screams in protest as I crash to the ground.

The red glow of brake lights flare and the bus screeches to a stop. Kotah vaults through the opening, his powerful legs reaching for me as his paws take purchase on the ground and his muscled shoulders absorb the drop. He hits the ground running, fangs bared.

More mouths take hold of me. Sharp teeth cut through the fluffy padding of my robe and clamp onto my shoulder and arm. I scream, twisting to untie the belt, trying to see—oh gawd—I'm being dragged into a farm field by a pack of wild-eyed hyenas.

Two of the slobbering beasts drop back to take on Kotah.

Their taunting yips and grunts hold none of the primal intelligence of my guys: a wolf's fierce growl, a jaguar's possessive roar, the keening shriek of a hawk's rage, and in the distance the raging snarl of my bear.

Hawk is airborne, his massive wings pumping hard to clear the field and close the distance between us. With the power of multiple hyenas running, my upper body is suspended in the air as my legs bump and crash over uneven land. I jostle and jolt, clamping my jaw tight to keep from biting my tongue.

It takes a moment for my hamster to climb back in its wheel. I'm still holding the gun Hawk gave me.

Yee-fucking-ha.

I twist and shoot, not caring about my aim. Everyone I care about is behind me. There's no threat of friendly fire. I fight the bump and drag and fire again. This time, one of the beasts yelps and the hold on my left shoulder drops away.

Men rush forward from the farmhouse ahead. They're dressed in all black and have guns raised. It's an ambush.

Another shot rings out and Kotah yelps behind me. His footing falters and I know by his sideways stagger, he's hit. It doesn't stop him. His paws still rip up the earth as he fights to get to me.

Bile burns the back of my tongue as the fur on my wolf's shoulder darkens. A rush of nausea hits as I watch his gait get progressively more uneven. The sickening sensation morphs to a hot rage boiling my blood in my veins.

These people want to hurt us—want to take my

guardians from me. I tighten my grip on the gun and twist.

*Tat-tat-tat-tat…* I unload the rest of the ammunition in a spray of bullets as fiery rage explodes inside me. My harem-scarem firing either injures or alarms my kidnappers.

I flop to a jerking halt and crack the back of my head on the clumpy dirt of the field. Dragging in a steadying breath, I connect with the raw power vibrating in my cells and accept who I'm meant to be. My guardians deserve more than forever putting their lives on the line to protect me.

*You are responsible for saving yourself. Always.*

Riley is right. I must protect myself.

As I feel my insides grow molten-hot, I drop the gun and force myself to stand. My balance is unsteady, but I curl my fingers into fists and get my head in the game.

*Come on, Calli girl. You can do this. You own this shit.*

*Kotah*

I've almost caught up to Calli when she shucks her robe and explodes into a fiery storm. Even shot, bleeding, and sick with worry, I can't help but suck in a breath of amazement. She truly is incredible. As her body explodes into a fiery blaze, she Banshee screams and turns on our attackers.

Maybe Hawk's right and she hasn't mastered her final form yet, but she's no less awe-inspiring as a woman aflame. When Jaxx blows past me on all fours, I realize my front leg is almost lame. The meat of my shoulder is on fire and I can't feel my right paw.

Still, I take the castoffs from Calli's shooting spree and rip out the throats of three hyena bastards as I hobble behind the group. If nothing else, I'll secure the rear.

I'm finishing up with the third when a wave of dizzy hits and I topple to the ground. I can't… I must help…

I turn my maw and vomit in the grass.

Damn. That can't be good.

*Brant*

Doc and I are almost caught up to the others when the kid goes down. There's no missing the scent of wolf blood in the air, but with Calli in the crosshairs, I don't have time to check him out. In mid-stride, I let off a guttural roar and swing my head toward Kotah lying in the bloody dirt. Thankfully, Doc gets my meaning and drops back to tend to the kid.

Jaxx is on the scene and the jaguar is a freaking phenom in battle. As an enforcer, I've worked and fought—with and against—hundreds of warriors. Jaxx stands out in that company, which is damn impressive.

Fast as lightning and lethal with his claws, our golden boy first responder earns new respect as he cuts a bloody swath through wildlings and men alike to secure our mate.

Hawk bypasses the obstacle of fighting through a wall of beasts by soaring above. When he catches up to Calli and begins his descent, a harrowing screech rents the air. He's knocked tumbling beak over tail-feathers, bombarded by two golden eagles. He recovers quickly and then talons bared, the three dive and claw and bat at one another.

Hawk won't get to our girl anytime soon.

I push hard, my muscles burning with the massive supply of energy I expend. Power ripples through my limbs and I realize my strength has bolstered with the connection of the others. Is that part of the mating?

I file that away to ask the kid later. Still, I feel them.

Kotah is struggling. Jaxx is wild. Hawk is pissed. And Calli is… filled with fiery confidence that ignites my own.

Despite them shooting at her, she's not getting hit. It must be the sheer molten heat she's giving off. She's melting the bullets before they get close enough to do her damage.

It's more than that, though. She's not afraid of what she's becoming like she was last time in the clearing. Facing a force of men and animals closing ranks, she's testing out her newfound form, stretching her boundaries to see what she can do.

Fuck yeah. She is a goddamn phoenix and these assholes are going to regret ever messing with her.

Good girl.

I snap the neck of a jackal and watch my girl in action. With a dozen, heavily armed men positioned ahead of her, she reaches back like a pitcher on a mound. When she shifts her weight forward and throws her arm, a hot, streaming blast of fire shoots from her palm. She's a fucking flamethrower and leaves nothing but a row of screaming men charred and twisting as their bodies burn.

I roar with pride.

Hawk shrieks above and somehow, I hear the

warning in his call. What? Why is he—*Shit.* From the loft of the barn, some cocklicker has a missile launcher pointed and ready—

I have no time to react. The weapon dislodges and the projectile hits Calli square in the chest. It knocks her fifty feet back and smack into the middle of a farmer's pond.

Hawk goes after the shooter's face, and Jaxx and I race to the water's edge. The jaguar doesn't hesitate. He goes from a full-on four-legged sprint into a hail Mary dive. He shifts mid-air and breaks the water's surface with his hands over his head in a perfect dive.

"Come on, Jaxx," I say, shifting back to being a man. I want to be out there. I want to help find Calli under the icy mirk of the water, but bears have an incredibly dense body mass and I can't swim. If I go in there, I'll sink and then Jaxx will be playing Baywatch to two of us. "Come on, Jaguar. Prove you're the man I think you are."

# CHAPTER ELEVEN

*Calli*

I wake to Jaxx's warm lips on my icy mouth—except, it isn't sensual. He blows a burst of oxygen into my lungs and I sputter and cough. Water spews up the back of my throat. It burns in my nose and my eyes water. After curling on the ground in a wicked coughing spree, I groan and fall limp on the grassy bank of a pond. "Gawd, it tastes like cat assholes and frat boy vomit made a disgusting lovechild in my mouth."

Jaxx pulls me off the ground and into his arms. Despite my warning of the worst morning breath evah, he kisses me again—for reals this time. When he pulls back, I see the pain and fear he's holding in check.

"I'm fine." I cup his scruffy jaw in the palm of my hand. Between nearly dying, recuperating, and now fighting, he's a bit more lumberJaxx rugged than when we first met. "Thanks for the save. How'd we do?"

His worry clears, washed away by his glorious crooked smile. "Point goes to the good guys. Hawk's got his people on cleanup. Kotah's being treated by Doc on the bus. And Brant and I are unbelievably happy to see your eyes open. You scared us, kitten."

My body quakes violently, racked by a super-sized shiver. "Where did all my heat go?"

"You were rocket-launched into the icy pond," Jaxx says. "How are you feeling?"

"Like I went from being Firestar, badass crime-fighter, to Olaf in Frozen."

"Here." Brant peels his shirt off and Jaxx helps me sit up. "I don't think you need a cooling-off period this time, beautiful. Your skin's like ice."

The two of them help me into the t-shirt which is massive and toasty and smells like Brant. I curl in on myself and moan from the decadence. The movement makes me wince and I press a gentle hand against the ache in my sternum. "Um, ow. That hurts."

Brant scoops me out of Jaxx's hold and pulls me against his broad, bare chest. His arms are strong around me and he carries me like I weigh no more than a child. His bear rumbles against my ear in approval as I snuggle closer into his warmth.

"Considering the dozens of bullets flying at you did nothing, I'm not surprised they pulled out the big guns. But damn, Calli, that asshole targeted you with a rocket launcher. Do you know how lucky we are that you're only saying ow?"

I nuzzle into the crook of his neck and close my eyes. I never noticed it before, but the big guy is a walking space heater. With the adrenaline of the battle drained away, exhaustion grips me. "Can we ignore the world and call a mental health day? I could bask in your heat and sleep for a week."

Jaxx squeezes my foot as we walk. "You did

amazing, kitten. You called that shift on intentionally. You are a natural. With a little training, you'll build up your endurance and be kicking ass in no time."

I yawn and close my eyes. "Thank you, boys."

Brant kisses the top of my wet hair. "You're welcome. We all survived, and you were spectacular."

"Yeah," Jaxx says. "With a hot shower and a mountain of blankets, you'll feel good as new in no time."

*Brant*

It's late when I push the bedroom door open a crack to check on my mate. She's lying in the center of the king-sized bed at the back of the bus, wrapped around our healing wolf, and has Jaxx spooning her from behind. The jaguar is lost in dreamland and I don't know if his state of total unconsciousness is residual exhaustion from his concussion or the pleasure of cuddling with Calli. I'll bet my balls all-in on the latter.

Either way, they look locked down for the night, so I ease back to let them—

"I'm not sleeping," Calli whispers, pushing up from the mattress to prop on her elbow. She's still wearing my t-shirt and hot-damn it hits me straight in the cock to see her thighs peeking out from the— "Are you all right?"

"Yeah, why?"

"Your eyes are practically glowing gold."

I swallow and pull back on the reins of my hunger for her. "Don't worry about that. I'm fine."

"What about Doc and Lukas?"

To say that she and Doc didn't hit it off would be the understatement of the year. With anyone else, I'd think the inquiry was empty lip-service, but with our connection strengthening, I feel her genuine concern. "All good, beautiful." I wink and head into the bathroom. "Let me wash up and I'll catch you up."

Blood doesn't bother me. As an FCO enforcer, I come home from work covered in blood or ichor or some form of disgusting bodily substance on the daily. Tonight is different. I don't want any part of those men affecting Calli's life any more than they already have.

Hawk and I worked them over for an hour to see what we could find out. It got messy. Still, none of them would connect the dots to either Darkside or the Black Knight.

I grab a bar of soap and get to work.

Exiting the bathroom, I pat my face and arms dry and hang the damp towel over the back of the little desk chair. As I draw nearer, the wolf rouses from where he's sleeping beside our girl and moves to the end of the bed. After walking a circle, he curls up in a ball, flicks his ear, and closes his eyes.

Good lad. "Thanks, buddy. Heal quickly, my man."

Calli lifts the covers, inviting me to lay with her. I swallow and raise a brow. "Yeah? You sure?"

Whatever she's sensing from me makes her smile. "Am I sure that I'm willing to share this giant mattress while we rest. Yes, Bear. I'm sure."

I chuckle. Normally I sleep in the buff but figure that might be ballsy, so I drop my jeans and keep my boxers firmly in place when I slide in beside her.

Calli's gaze catches the bulging evidence of what's doing behind the thin layer of cotton and her mouth drops open. "Is all that for little ole *me?*"

I slide into the warmth of her blanket cocoon and cuddle her close to my chest. To avoid pushing my luck, I keep my hips pulled back far enough that my straining need for her remains left to her imagination… for now.

"You are perfection in my arms, beautiful." I draw her scent deep into my lungs and try to reconcile the past few days. This female, who seems tiny and fragile, is the kick-ass other half to my soul. Her delicate air is a stunning illusion. Calli is whiskey in a teacup—a fierce spirit in a dainty package.

The devotion I felt for her, at first sight, was magic—a destiny taking hold. That feeling pales to what has bloomed after two days of getting to know her.

I kiss her temple and sigh, contented like I never knew I could be. She blinks up at me with a half-masted gaze, a sappy, sleepy smile softening her face. Right. She asked me about my erection, and I got lost in her eyes.

"Yes, it's for you. Take anything you want from me whenever you want it, but tonight you called a PG sleepover, and I agree. It's a good idea. You are in desperate need of rest to regain your strength. And you'll need it. We start training tomorrow."

She nuzzles against my chest and reaches over my side to hug me. The velvet warmth of her touch barely wraps over my ribs. She blinks up at me, a sweet smile crossing her lips. "I'm also in desperate need of a bear hug."

"Then it's a good thing you have one handy." I squeeze her tighter and press my lips against her forehead. Damn, with my cock throbbing with a pulse of its own and my bear wild with the need to be claimed, I'm getting dangerous.

I need inside Calli more than I need blood in my veins and air in my lungs. I need her to need me. I squeeze my eyes shut and lock my shit down. "Close your eyes, beautiful. When we wake up, we'll be at the Bastion and can regroup."

*Hawk*

I lean back in the private cubicle I'm using as an office and eye the bedroom door at the back of the bus. Calli and the others hunkered down for the night about an hour ago and I feel their bonds tightening—to one another.

Not me.

Not that I care. I never wanted to be tied to this mess, so there's no reason to feel slighted because I'm the one on the outside looking in. Whatever the universe had in store when we matched up as the perfect other halves for each other, something critical got lost in translation.

My passions run hot for elegant brunettes who know to be seen and not heard and bow when I give the order. I like them submissive and detached—no exaggerated expectations or demands on my time.

Calli's none of that—and never will be.

I'm a man who allows no complications with my sex life and Calli and this phoenix guardian quint is the motherfucking Titanic of complications.

The universe is wrong.

The only reason I can't get Spitfire out of my mind is bonding magic. Otherwise, I'd be fucking Jayne or the next anonymous female that catches my eye.

Even saying the words in my head, I hear the lie.

No. It's not a lie. It's desperation. I haven't had sex in almost a week and for me, that's two lifetimes. That's all it is. If I take the edge off, I'll see things clearly again. My cock has been a solid rod of granite, day and night, for days. I need a break from the incessant drive to mate.

Right. Easing the chair away from the desk surface, I reach back, dim the light, and close the door. The *click* of the lock brings on an almost Pavlovian surge of anticipation in my pants.

Yeah, yeah. It's back to teenaged basics. Let off the pressure and I'll be good. Since I go commando, it's as simple as me toeing off my shoes and setting my folded pants and shirt on the desk.

Manspreading naked in the desk chair, I tilt back and glare up at the ceiling. Why have I been reduced to this? A morning stroke off in the shower to get the day started on the right foot is one thing. Seeking release in a moving closet while four others are soaking up all the warm fuzzies in the next room is quite another.

Yeah, well… desperate times.

Oh, for fuck's sake, I need to get this done already.

I swipe a hand over my pec and twist the platinum hoop pierced through my nipple. The assault sends a sharp tingle across my nerve endings and my already stiff cock jumps against my abs. I focus on the expansion of my lungs, the steady beat of my heart.

Closing my eyes, I send my palm downward, over the ridged planes of my six-pack to the problem at hand. My skin is hot and smooth, stretched over honed muscles. I dip south for a second and squeeze my sac. My balls are so tight, they feel like they might burst from the pressure.

*Dammit.* Somewhere over the passing days, the urge to release increased way beyond an annoying ache. We're now in flat out need territory.

I need this.

I grip my shaft and the contact is electric. A moan rumbles out of my chest as my erection kicks in my hand. *Shit*, that feels good. I start a slow tugging rhythm and sink into the sensation. This. This is basic biology.

I arch as I continue to touch myself. Without invitation, erotic images of Calli in the backseat of my truck invade my moment. Naked and horny, she pressed the rounds of her breasts against the kid's chest and rode his bulge until she shattered.

*Fuck me. It's… so good.*

My breath tightens in my chest. I grip tighter and pick up speed. The feminine sound she made as the pressure built. The intoxicating scent of her core weeping for attention…

*Oh, fuck… Faster. Harder.*

When the quiet *click-click-click* of my rhythm breaks the silence of my jack off, I glance down at the glistening head of my engorged cock. Precum rises through the opening, slicking my crown…

*Oh fuck.* I throw my head back, the reward of release pulsing in my balls but refusing to come. I'm suspended at the edge of the most glorious pleasure, my entire body tight with hunger. I focus on the steady *click-click* of tossing hard with cum leaking from my tip.

It's so good. I need this so badly.

My balls are on fire, they tighten and lock, quivering with the need to fucking let loose. "Yes," I pant. Sweat drips off my chin and down my chest. I hammer at myself with a pounding rhythm my load bursting to gain freedom.

"Yes, fuck… please."

I'm back in my truck again, watching Calli masturbate on the kid. Fuck I want that to be me. I want to tie her up and fuck her for hours. I want my face at her core lapping at that incredible scent. I want my cock so deep inside her that when I come, my scent covers her inside and out.

The movie in my mind shifts. Calli's look of devastation and betrayal set up shop in my head.

*"Stop!"* She swipes at the moisture dripping off her chin and pulls a labored breath. *"You think you have me figured out, but maybe you're not as smart as you think you are."*

I laugh in the face of her destruction. *"You're nothing special Calli and you know it. Our world needs greatness right now. Hard truth time—that isn't you."*

My words haunt me now. Yes, I spoke them to save Jaxx's life, but regret won't knit that damage back together.

Guilt cuts me so deeply, it feels like my heart is cleaving in two. I have no right to find pleasure using Calli as my mental prop. That wasn't my intention, but despite intentions and my protestations, our little Spitfire got under my skin.

I sigh, staring down at my quickly deflating cock.

Damn it. Can't one thing go right for me?

What the fuck do I do now?

# CHAPTER TWELVE

*Calli*

I wake in a loose tangle of sheets beneath lazy swaths of white gossamer. The delicate draping of the canopy above swings free, billowing like enchanted ghosts protecting their guest from the outside world. I peer through the sheer veil at the warm, honey-stained post and beam architecture and leaded, stained-glass windows. Beyond the end of the bed, a stone wall rises from the hardwood floors and houses a fireplace dividing the bedroom from a great room beyond.

"Good morning, sleeping beauty."

I glance behind me and find Jaxx sitting against the headboard watching me sleep. "How'd I get here?"

"You were out cold when we arrived early this morning. Hawk had the cabin arranged. Brant carried you in. And *voila*, here you are."

Even though it's only been a couple of days since I woke up in the safehouse, it feels like a lifetime has passed. I stretch, arching my back, and roll over to face Jaxx. "And this is the Bastion?"

"The surrounding compound, not the castle used for the business center. The Bastion is the heart of the fae community, laws, and government. People come and go often, so there are cabins and lodges for gathering outside the gates. That's where we are."

"Well, they have a welcoming taste."

"We aim to please."

Jaxx is clean-shaven this morning and looking damn fine in graphite dress slacks and a black V-neck that pulls tight over his landscape. There's no tension in his shoulders and all evidence of his injury is gone. I'm beyond relieved. "You're looking super sexy this morning."

"You like?"

*Mhmm*, yeah, I do. The tremendous yearning I feel at the closeness of him overwhelms me. I roll over and reach under the bottom edge of his shirt to find the fastener of his pants. When I look up, his wild, turquoise gaze burns into mine. "Tell me we don't have to rush straight into introductions and training schedules."

He brushes his thumb across my lips, and I give it a gentle bite. "I suppose we could take a moment. After all, you are the star of the show. You get to have your say."

"And what are the odds that I can have my way with you and not set the cabin on fire?"

Jaxx's low, throaty chuckle does something sinful to my insides. "The odds are good. You called your phoenix forth during the ambush. That means you're gainin' control. I bet, with me as a sexual outlet, you'll be fine."

"Good." I drop his zipper to reveal the golden hue of his skin beneath. I crawl up his legs and press my lips low on his bare abdomen. "If you want these pretty clothes to survive, you need to get naked now. I'm still a little shaken about almost losing you and need some private time to reassure myself that we're good."

Jaxx is naked and pushing Brant's t-shirt up my thighs and over my head in seconds. My hair falls in a tumbling cascade to rest on my breasts and his gaze is locked. "We're more than good."

"Good, because I'm crazy randy."

Jaxx laughs and tosses my nightie. "Your wild side is strong this morning, is she?" He grips me by the hips and yanks me down the bed. It's rough and playful and I squeal under his control. He lowers his face to my breasts and nuzzles them like the feline he is. His tongue is hot and is soon driving me mad.

He lets off a raspy purr. It tightens in my core and I almost orgasm. Big cats don't purr—but this one does.

"How sexy is that?"

"Oh, kitten. You ain't seen nothin' yet." Jaxx circles my nipple with his tongue and the purring returns.

Gawd, I want him. The craving is growing stronger by the minute. I gasp, twisting as his hand slides around my hip and down my belly. His fingers inch toward the slick heat of my folds and I suck in a breath. "I've never been this horny."

A rush of heat meets his fingers at my core.

"Frack, you're wet."

"Told you."

The next minutes pass in a ravishing flurry of hands and mouths and tongues. Jaxx's instincts are perfect—as if he senses my need and can anticipate what I want.

Maybe he can. There's so much I don't understand about our mating bond.

I think about the four of them and wonder what characteristics convinced the universe they are the perfect match for me. Nakotah, my omega, is smart, innocent, and the most emotionally sensitive of the four. He's the calm in this storm.

Then there is Brant. Overprotective and smothering one minute and a comedic charmer the next. He's brute strength, fearless, and loyal. The easiest fit for what I imagine a Guardian of the Phoenix to be.

"Oh, Jaxx," I breath, bucking my hips so his fingers slide deeper inside me. "I need you. Right now."

His laughter vibrates against my nipple, but he doesn't stop. He nips at the tight tip and I shudder.

Jaxx, my sexy jaguar, is a lead by example kinda guy—calm, direct, and steadfast. He's a paranormal paramedic by trade, so he's a nurturer… a fixer.

That leaves Hawk… my shrewd and ruthless one. The loner. The mate who holds himself above the others. Even thinking about what he did to me ignites a fire in my chest. He hurt me—but like he said, 'It takes one to know one.'

Because of him, Jaxx is here with me now.

Jaxx pulls away from my breast with a wet *pop* and I instantly miss the connection. I twist, grinding my thigh against his cock like a horny cat on a scratching post.

The predatory growl that rumbles between us, hits me right between my legs. His gaze narrows. "You're sure? You're feeling better about things?"

"I am." I swallow getting lost in the pools of his

warm turquoise eyes. "I'm so hot and hungry. It's insane… not to mention damned distracting."

Jaxx nips at the tender flesh of my sternum and shifts to pay homage to my other breast. "That's a wildling thing. Our primal 'F' needs rage paramount—food, fighting, and especially fucking."

"Yes, please. Last one first." I arch against his touch tilting my pelvis to give him more access. The pad of his forefinger glides over my throbbing clit and I shudder. "And the sooner the better."

Jaxx props himself up on his palms, prowling over me like a predator. I miss his fingers, and whimper, so aching and empty. The scent of our lust is heavy in the air and I wonder how far it carries. In a community of heightened senses, this could get embarrassing.

His gaze grows serious as he brushes his lips over mine. "Calli, I don't want you to rush. There's plenty of time."

"Now's a great time."

Jaxx chuckles. "Then teach me who you are behind closed doors. I'm getting a dominant wild child vibe. Do you like your man to talk dirty or have you got a filthy mouth yourself? I want to learn you."

My cheeks heat. On one hand, I feel very exposed sexually attacking this gorgeous man. On the other, I'm desperate to get to the fucking. We're eye to eye, only inches apart. I swallow and find my voice. "Right now, I ache. I want this thick cock,"—I say, gripping his bobbing erection—"Inside me. Less talking. More orgasming."

Jaxx lowers himself over me and I wrap my legs

around his hips, arching off the mattress with the ache of my clenching core. The friction of his hard against my wet is so good my orgasm pushes forward.

The keening of sensation is raw. So good. We aren't even having sex yet and my breath is catching in throaty bursts.

Jaxx's skin is hot, a stark contrast to the cool air of the room that teases over my flesh. My nipples are still peaked and Jaxx inhales a long, unsteady breath. There's a look of raptured amazement on his face. "You're so, fucking delicious. I can't wait to devour you."

My breath catches. How can any man want me as desperately as Jaxx's expression suggests he does? What makes me worthy? He barely knows me? I barely know *him*. I stiffen and he draws a steadying breath.

"Too much? You okay?"

I shake my head. "I, uh… I have condoms in my purse but have no idea where it is. I'm wondering, praying really, that we don't have to stop."

Jaxx winks and positions his erection. "I've got you covered with wildling magic. Without getting into a biology lesson right this minute, trust me. I will take care of you."

And I do.

Before I catch it, a girly squeal bubbles up my throat. I don't know what it is about him, but my entire body is alive. "Excellent. Now, back to business. Your female aches."

Jaxx laughs, drops his mouth to my neck, and presses his hips. The penetration halts as the head of his cock pushes forward. He stretches me open and energy explodes between us.

Our bond courses between us, swirling from my system to his and back again. The connection links us. Two are now one. We are together, complete.

Fire licks over my skin and moves to cover him. He doesn't burn or wince. He does cry out, but not from pain.

He thrusts his hips forward, fully penetrating me as he throws his head back. My need for him increases a hundredfold. It's torture. Succulent. Erotic torture.

"Oh, gawd," I pant, writhing beneath him as his hips start to pump. "What's happening. I've never been this turned on."

"You're tightly wound, kitten," Jaxx says, his voice a deep bass, with his purr. "You need a little mate TLC."

I groan as he inches farther inside me. He's big but I'm wet and greedy. There's no issue with priming me for an invasion. Back arched, I bear down, and the sharp heat of my release burns hotter. *A little TLC?*

"If this is mating. I need a lot."

"A lot it is." Jaxx thrusts his hips forward and we both cry out. He stills as I adjust. This is what I want, to be possessed by him, taken, deliciously stretched.

I'm new to the whole scent thing, but the air is rife with a seductive mix of need and pheromones and magic. Jaxx lowers his mouth to mine and I'm lost. A flick of his tongue. A gentle pinch of teeth trapping my lip. Whatever is happening it is life-altering… and not enough.

I wriggle, grabbing his shoulders, bucking my hips. There's nothing ladylike about the way I claw at him, pulling him closer, urging him to drive me insane.

Thankfully, the torture is over. He draws back, and pushes deeper, once, twice… "Yes."

The moist glide of our joining is ecstasy revisited again and again. Harder. Faster. He throws his shoulders back and leverages his weight to slam his hips. I look at him from under heavy eyelids. He's so beautiful, his lip dotted with sweat, his jaw clenched tight.

I'm so exquisitely stretched my body ripples around his cock, squeezing and trembling with my impending orgasm. I let off a moan that surely carries beyond this room.

Lost as I am, I don't care who hears.

"Come for me, kitten," Jaxx's voice rasps with need as he pumps into me. "Cream my cock so I can keep fucking you for hours."

*Hours… oh yes.* Wild for him, I pull his mouth to mine and rock hard against his thrusts. My orgasm explodes through me, starting with the erotic spasms of my core and radiating out until my entire body convulses. Yes… gawd, *yes!*

He watches me as I fall apart, his possessive gaze more animal than man. I ride out the violent waves of release and something inside me unlocks.

My mind spirals. "You are mine."

"All yours," he says, his voice rough. "As you are mine."

*Jaxx*

Calli is hands down the sexiest female I ever had the pleasure of worshipping. With her golden hair sweated out and sticking to the rounds of full, swaying breasts, and her breath coming in heaving gasps—she's incredible. And the fact that she wants to claim me as her own…

The burn of release twists in my balls and explodes. I throw my head back and lose track of reality. My body explodes into her, utterly shatters. A surge of possession hits me as my cum fills her in hot streams.

This female—the phoenix—is *mine.*

Mating heat has my jaguar roaring within.

As her orgasm fades, she slows her grinding and catches her breath. Her smile lights me up. Shit. So goddamn sexy. She collapses beneath me and I roll to the side to cover her with a sheet, so she doesn't catch a chill.

"Wow," she says, chuckling against the racing thrum of my heartbeat. Her gaze flips from hazy ecstasy to assessing me. "Are you okay?"

In truth, I'm off-balance and my stomach is so empty it's cannibalizing itself, but who the hell cares. "I'm amazing. Thank you for asking." Her smile fades as she studies my face. I roll over and stroke her cheek. "What's wrong, kitten? Too much? Are you sore?"

"No. I, uh… I want you to know, I don't usually do this." She gestures between us. "Despite what we just did and what Hawk said, I'm not a wild child. I've had a handful of men in my bed and only ever guys I was committed to."

I nod and kiss her shoulder. "You don't have to explain your past to me, Calli."

She leans in and kisses me, gentle and sweet. "I

want you to understand this means something to me. It's more than mating hormones and a wildling need for sex. I hunger for you, Jaguar—no question—but more than that, I'm falling for you. You're a good man with strong morals, and a kind, forgiving heart. You're protective and loyal and gorgeous and I'm so grateful you found me and have taken such good care of me."

Oh, sweet mercies. This female is too much.

I swallow and try to breathe past the weight pressing on my chest. "It means more to me too, kitten. Wildlings mate for life and my animal claimed you from that first moment. You don't understand the extent of what that means yet, but you will. I'm all-in here, Calli. I am your pride now."

She sinks into my arms, tracing a gentle circuit over my chest and down my arm. On the third trip toward my elbow, she props her head on her hand. "Was that normal sex for a wildling?"

I laugh. It's a shallow, breathy sound because I haven't gotten reacquainted with oxygen. "No. That was… I can't even." I search my vocabulary for a word that might begin to cover what happened. "Transcendent."

Calli laughs and I'm struck stupid. With her guard down and her body sated and relaxed, she is radiant. "I thought so too. I have no idea where that came from."

Now it's my turn to smile. "That's mating heat. It'll be like that with each of us and all of us. The five of us bonding seemed crazy to you looking at it from a human viewpoint a few days ago, but once you wrap your head around how the fae world works, you'll see. It'll be amazing."

Calli flings her arm up and covers her eyes. “How will I ever survive four of you.”

I roll her onto her back and press her into the mattress. “There’s only me here now. And so far, no fires.”

Her face lights up and I see the moment her attention shifts back to sex. “And you did say something about fucking me for hours.”

I chuckle and pull her closer. “I certainly did.”

# CHAPTER THIRTEEN

*Brant*

"How's the feline?" I ask Doc when he returns to the billiard's room in the main lodge of the Bastion compound. When he finished giving the kid a clean bill of health, he headed to our cabin to check on Jaxx. The jaguar barely recovered from head trauma before getting thrown straight into a roadside battle. Doc's concern about a patient's well-being is nothing new. The guy is solidly good people. He also has a weird expression screwing up his face as he reclaims his cue and studiously chalks the felt tip. "What? I thought with the flood of tears Calli laid on him, Jaxx is good to go."

Doc chuckles. "Oh, he's good to go all right. I'd say he's made a full recovery."

The subtext of what he isn't saying raises my hackles. "What? What's the face?"

He grabs the triangle to rack us up and shakes his head. "Not my story to tell. Let's say, my medical skills are no longer required."

I may not be the Rhodes Scholar our wolf is, but I'm a far cry from stupid. Jaxx seemed steady last night. Phoenix tears are the bomb. Closing my eyes, I focus on the growing bond between the five of us. I find Hawk's energy agitated and alone on the grounds, Nakotah is reading in the library, and Jaxx and Calli are—my bear growls.

"Oh, *that's* what you mean."

Doc raises an ebony brow. "Yep. That's what I mean."

It's not like I see or hear what's going on across the compound, but I pick up on the sensations. Jaxx has recovered and is making up with Calli in the most intimate of ways. I chuckle and set my attention back on the game.

"You're not jealous?" Doc asks, lining up his shot. "I figured the way your bear claimed her, knowing what's going on would set you off."

I amble around to the other side of the table. "Do I envy Jaxx his moment? Without a doubt. Do I feel angry or jilted? Nope. Not at all."

Doc shakes his head as if he finds that hard to believe.

"Seriously. Jaxx claimed Calli first and they have some guilt and trust issues to work past after the accident. A win for him is a win for all of us. The jaguar's smart. He'll treat our girl right."

"By what I witnessed, there's no question about that. Your girl has lungs."

The growl that rumbles from my chest is nothing I can control. "Watch it, Doc."

He raises his palms looking confused. "Touchy."

"Calli isn't like the other girls, Doc. This mating bond… I can't describe it. When she speaks, the hair on my arms stands on end. My pulse races when I catch her scent in the air. Calli is the sun in my universe and I can't imagine it's any different for the others."

His dark eyes are lit with skepticism, but I don't care. He doesn't understand. "And what happens when the hormones settle, and the honeymoon phase fades? You're committing yourself to a five-way relationship with people you've known for a week. I'm worried, Bear. I know you. Forever has never entered your picture. You live for the moment."

"And I had a great decade doing it. It's different now. It's more like—"

Kotah joins us, book in hand and stops inside the entrance to the games room. "Apologies, am I interrupting? Should I come back?"

"Nah, come here, buddy." I wave him over and lay my arm across his shoulders to face Doc. I've got over a foot of height and a hundred and twenty pounds on the kid, but he fits against my side like he was born to be there.

Doc's eyes widen and I know he doesn't understand.

"As much as I love the bears of our sleuth—and I do, never doubt that—Calli, Kotah, Jaxx, and maybe even at some level Hawk are my family now. They are my heart. It's not about hormones and mating, though I look forward to that. It's a sense of belonging, of knowing that if we take the time and make the effort, the five of us are destined to become something incredible."

I glance down at the sweet surprise on Kotah's face. The dip of his chin tells me we're on the same page. I don't know a lot about the kid's upbringing yet, but I get the sense that he hasn't always gotten the support and acceptance he needs.

That's over now. He's mine as much as Calli and the others. "At least that's how I feel."

Before it gets weird, I ruffle the kid's hair and set him free. "See, this is nothing but a good thing, Doc. Don't worry about me. I'm fucking overjoyed. Once we find our rhythm, this quint will be legendary."

As the words solidify in the air between us, I'm even more certain. Yeah, when it comes to laying down roots, it's Musketeer time—all for one and one for all.

Kotah recovers from whatever emotional rush he got from my PDA and nods. I don't know if it's our mating bond or an effect from him being an omega, but I adore him and will give my life to protect him from anyone who might do him harm.

*Mine.*

Doc will not understand that, so I move on. I point to the book clutched under the kid's arm and nod. "Go ahead, buddy. Did you find something you want to share?"

*Hawk*

"The stylist called," Lukas says. "She's compiling the items you requested for tonight's gala and will have them to the cabin this afternoon. The updated files on the other guardians are in your inbox. And you're scheduled to appear in front of the Fae Council at the end of the regular session this afternoon at 3:15. I entered it into your schedule."

"And access to the satellite system?"

"Approved, but you'll need to go in person. They

had a potential breach with remote access and until they isolate the source, it's hands-on only."

Inconvenient, but understandable. "Okay, what about the coroner's report on the dead women from the drow property?"

"At first blush, it seems they died of heart failure."

I blink up at him and frown. "Mass, simultaneous heart failure? That's impossible. What was their blood chemistry?"

"The lab is breaking down an unknown substance found in all of them. They're not sure what it is, but it seems to have caused unusually low levels of tryptophan and erratically high levels of adrenaline."

"To what end?"

"Other than death?"

"Yes, other than that."

"Undetermined at this point."

"All right. What about the establishment where Calli's friend tended bar? Any luck tracking down the leader of the Sovereign Sons or their guns buyer?"

"Nothing yet."

"And the men who ambushed us?"

"Nothing yet."

"Any hits on this Black Knight fellow?"

"Nothing yet."

"What about the reason for the rise of the phoenix?" I raise a finger and point at him. "If you say, 'Nothing yet,' I will gut you."

Lukas stares at me and purses his lips, saying nothing.

"For fuck's sake! What do I pay you for? Have you got any answers about anything?"

He shrugs undeterred. "You were right about the discrepancy on the maps provided for the land contract. The science team concluded that the shift in the waterway didn't occur naturally but was coerced by damming and digging about ten years ago. Someone wanted the river shifted."

"Ten years ago? Why? Who benefits from the shift?"

"Jayne's working on that."

My phone rings and I sigh. Speak of the she-devil. "Hold on a second." I put the call on hold and go back to my conversation with Lukas. "Check the dark web for any references to this Black Knight or anything to do with Darkside. Keep on it. Maybe one day we'll find we have more answers than questions."

"Where there's life, there's hope."

When Lukas clears the room, I accept the call and rub the growing ache in my temple. "Jayne. What can I do for you?"

*Jaxx*

After an amazing wake-up session with Calli, we shower and eventually end up getting dressed—eventually. I understand the day is ticking away and the guys are waiting but being naked with my mate and having her to myself is the most consuming sensation I ever have experienced.

It's not uncommon in our world but with our rocky start, for a minute there, I wondered if it would happen.

"Stop fidgeting." I slap her hand away from the lapel of her little jacket. Hawk sent her over a day outfit from the boutique in the main lodge and it is breathtaking.

No. She's breathtaking.

"I'm going to mess this up."

I check her position facing the stone fireplace and call up my parents for a video chat. "Just be yourself. My parents are awesome, and they'll love you."

Her whimper of defeat is so damned cute I can't stand it. I give her a quick kiss and check that she's ready.

"Jaxx, seriously. I'm going to say something stupid, pass out, or worse… what if I shoot fire out of my eyes."

I chuckle and step back from my dialing phone propped on the mantle. "That honestly wouldn't be the worst intro my parents have suffered through with the girls I've dated."

She's so unamused it's hilarious.

"Okay, if your eyeballs heat up, duck out of the frame and shoot fireballs into the hearth. No biggie."

She glares like I've grown a second head. Hilarious.

The phone rings and I pull her against my side so she can't escape. It rings… and continues ringing until the call is dropped. "Weird. I told them I was calling with exciting news. I wonder where they went."

I shrug off the disappointment of not being able to show off my girl and set her free. "Looks like you're off the hook."

"Thank the gods."

*Calli*

Jaxx is amazing, and I am sure his parents are amazing, but he can't grasp the scope of how different our lives have been. He grew up in a nuclear family, devoted parents, brilliant older sister, grand-parents, cousins, birthday parties, family dinners, the whole works. I try to picture it... and I've got nothing.

I send up a prayer of thanks to whatever fae gods saved me from making a fool of myself and alienating the people who mean the most to him.

It sounds selfish, I know, but I need a moment to process. Hell, we just got together five minutes ago. Give a girl a minute to adjust.

I, of course, say none of this aloud. Like I said, Jaxx is amazing. No way will I burst his afterglow by admitting I'm not ready to shout our mating news from the rooftops.

Instead, I link our fingers as we leave the cabin and tamp down my need to run for the hills. Of course, I won't get far in strappy slingback pumps.

Where I expected to wear yoga pants and a tank for training later, Hawk sent me a black sleeveless pantsuit with a chiffon overlay skirt and emerald bolero jacket to wear up to the main lodge. It's elegant, very pretty, and totally out of my comfort zone.

"You look stunning. The people here will be in awe of the phoenix before they even meet you. We'll get you fed and then go back to our cabin with the others to change and start the training we need to make up for."

We walk side-by-side, our steps in sync, our fingers

linked between us. The earthy smell of the forest hangs thick in the air and my pulse kicks up a notch. I've never been outdoorsy before, but I get the sense my phoenix likes having space to stretch her wings.

Maybe one day soon, I'll properly call my phoenix into a full shift and see what that feels like. I need to get a handle on that. The fae community is counting on me and I'm not ready.

I'm still thinking about that when a tiger bursts from the trees and races across the path ahead of us. He's swatting at a shrieking eagle, leaping ten feet into the air, swiping to catch the bird.

Whatever Jaxx sees in my face, makes him chuckle. "While wildlings mix and mingle across the country, the primary alpha center for each group is where most of us live. The canines in the north, the avians in the east, the felines in the south and the ursines in the west. We're an aggressive species and don't always get along. We stick to our quarters."

The breathy sounds of a private coming together draws my attention to a bench tucked under a weeping willow. A man is sitting on the bench naked with the woman in his lap riding his cock and another man kneeling in front of her, suckling her breasts.

"Some people are getting along fine." I watch, not meaning to intrude but fascinated by their freedom to express their hungers. It feeds a giddy pang of excitement building in me. It will be like this with my mates as we accept one another.

"Yeah, they seem to be doing just fine," Jaxx says.

The sun is almost completely overhead when we arrive at the main lodge. I'm swamped with the realization that with the heightened senses of the fae, everyone will know why we're so late.

Stupid super-sniffers. "Is your marking scent noticeable on me?"

"Fuck yeah." The predatory purr that rumbles from his chest vibrates squarely between my legs. He swings me around and pulls me against his solid chest. There's a playful fire in his eyes that ignited a few hours ago that calls to me. "No one in this compound will question who claimed you as his mate."

"That's both super sexy and offensive," I say, freeing myself from his arms before my hunger for him gets me into trouble. "I'm nobody's property."

He chuckles and swings our joined hands between us. "It's less about being someone's property and more about knowing who will rip their throat out if something happens to you. A male's mark puts other members of our world on notice, and it works both ways."

We arrive at a great, wooden lodge on the edge of a lake and Jaxx opens the gate for me. Three lion cubs and two roly-poly bear cubs are grunting and rolling in a fenced pen on the front lawn. The brunette woman watching them straightens as we approach.

"Wait for it…" Jaxx whispers beside me.

The woman eyes him up and down, making it very clear that she likes what she sees. Natch. She swallows, a soft smile curving her lips until we get about twenty feet from her. Then, everything about her demeanor changes and she stands down.

"Hello, Ginny," Jaxx says, stopping as we pass. "This is Calli. Calli, Ginny is my Alpha's niece. She takes care of the young here on the compound for visiting delegates."

"It's nice to meet you, Calli," the lynx feline says. She dips her chin to me and drops her gaze to the ground. "Welcome to the Bastion. I do hope you enjoy your stay."

"Thanks," I say, baffled. "It's nice to meet you too."

Jaxx's warm palm at the small of my back leads me through the double glass doors and into the lodge. Once inside, I take his hand and tug him to the side. "So, my scent on you does the same thing? Women smell our ode to sexy times, they know you're mine, and they'll mind their manners?"

He nods. "It's partly manners and partly respecting that you're dominant. Whether or not you've got control over your animal side, you are an alpha female of a very powerful and respected species. Females won't touch what's yours if they have half a brain."

He's watching my reaction and chuckles. "Like that, do you? A little possessive, are you, kitten?"

I link my arm with his and waggle my brows. "More than a little. We're together and building toward something. I'm glad women like her know it."

"That's all I'm saying.".

"There you are," Nakotah says, meeting us in the grand foyer. Dressed in traditional doe-skin pants and vest, he looks every bit the male of his heritage. His long, chestnut hair is drawn back and braided, and he wears a colorful beaded choker over the wide black leather of his usual one.

He kisses my hand and smiles. "You are

resplendent."

I'm not even sure what that means but I get the gist. I brush my finger over the beading on his throat and swallow. "You're killing it yourself, sweetie."

Jaxx told me we'd be in the lodge for a bit and then back to the cabin to change before working out. If all my guys are dressed to kill like this today, we may not make it out of the cabin after all.

Kotah draws a deep breath and blushes. "Right now, you need to eat, *Chigua*. The rest must wait, I'm afraid."

Jaxx chuckles as Kotah tugs me down the hall toward the mouth-watering aroma of grilled meat. "The wolf's right. It's long past the time when you should've eaten."

I hug Kotah's arm and slow down the race toward the kitchen. I'm used to sneakers not heels and I don't want to end up faceplanting in front of the elders of the fae world. "I'm fine. The morning just… got away on us."

I search Kotah's face. He's so guileless my heart trips looking at him. The last thing I want is to bring up my morning with Jaxx and hurt Kotah's feelings or make him feel left out—especially after how good he's been to me.

I squeeze his arm. "I'm sorry if it's weird for you knowing Jaxx and I spent the morning together?"

Kotah stops and brushes his fingers over the blush of my cheek. "Calli, we are to be a mated quint. You stand here smiling, more relaxed and sated than I've seen you in days. How can that be a bad thing?"

I swallow. "Well, it's not for *me*, but I want to make

sure there's no tension between you four and that no one feels left out. I want this to work for all of us."

Jaxx shakes his head. "You're still looking at things through a human mindset. The five of us are a pack, a clan, a unit. However you describe it, you thriving in this quint is our primary concern. It's more than our duty, it's our greatest pleasure. We may disagree and, knowing Hawk, likely come to blows, but it'll never be about you or your happiness."

Polyamory is foreign to me, but if this morning is an example of what it can be like with each or all of them, then, *hellooo*, I'll adjust. "I don't want anyone to feel slighted."

Kotah's braid brushes my wrist as he leans to whisper in my ear. It's a soft tickle and feels far too intimate for such a public setting. "Yes, Brant and I, and likely even Hawk, want more time with you, private or otherwise, but it's not at the expense of the others. As males, we yearn for a deep emotional connection with you. As animals, we hunger for the final quint claiming."

I search the depths of his brown eyes. "Final claiming?"

"Yes. Only when the five of us come together as one will our bond be truly complete."

"All five of us at once?" I say, my mouth going dry.

He holds up the book in his hand. "I spent the morning in the library. According to what I discovered. We can each be with you and our bond will grow but only when all of us are together will the extent of our powers unlock."

Despite my growing attraction to each of them, four

men at once sounds too exploitive and hedonistic. Besides, they don't even like Hawk. Sex for the sake of releasing powers isn't anything I want to be a part of.

How do I say that without disappointing them?

My stomach growls and I place a hand over my belly. "Okay, you're right. I need sustenance. Lead the way."

# CHAPTER FOURTEEN

*Calli*

After lunch, Brant, Jaxx, Kotah, and I head back to our cabin in the woods. Since I no longer have a phone, I had Kotah send Hawk a text inviting him to join us for our meal, but he didn't come, and he didn't respond. Knowing him, he's probably in a meeting or putting out a political fire somewhere. Still, I don't like the divide growing between us. Chronologically, it's been less than two days since he shredded me. In the grand scheme of my shifter evolution, it feels like years ago.

What if he's already gone to the elders to be severed from his bond? It's too soon. He hasn't given us a chance.

He hasn't given *me* a chance.

"In your dreams, Bear," Jaxx says, laughing as the four of us burst into the three-bedroom guest cabin. "Muscle mass is important, but it doesn't negate speed, agility, and cunning. Right, Kotah?"

Kotah nods. "Sorry, Brant. I'm with Jaxx on this."

Brant chuckles and his massive chest bounces with his amusement. "Of course, you are. You're a wolf. You gotta pair up with the jaguar. Just like you'll have to pair up if you expect to take me down."

I laugh and head into the bedroom. On the dresser, there is a pile of new clothes that weren't there when Jaxx and I left this morning. The closet door is open and there are several evening dresses and the corresponding shoes. I've suspected my personal shopper is Hawk all along.

Now I'm sure of it.

The guys are still joking and talking smack about how badly they intend to kick each other's respective asses when I grab a set of workout clothes and head to the bathroom. It's not that I'm shy, but I know damned well that if I'm naked in front of any one of them, I'm going to be lost to lust again and distracted from training.

I pad quickly and quietly across the suite until I'm at the bathroom door—

A sharpness of emotion twangs the tension of my connection to the guys and I stop. The mating bond is solidifying like an invisible cable connecting the five of us and whatever I'm sensing twists in my gut.

I abandon the door to the bathroom and continue down the hall to the office. Hawk sits on the edge of the desk, his back toward me. His shoulders are rigid, the spine of his black vest pulling at the seams. "I don't give a fuck," he growls in a throaty tone. "I pay you to get things done, so get it done."

The cellphone flings across the room and smashes to bits against the wall. He tips his head back and roars at the ceiling. I feel his animal writhing close to the surface and wonder what is testing his control.

I haven't figured out the tie we share or what it

means for us in the future, but Hawk's suffering aches in my chest. I'm still furious with him—there's no denying that—but more than wanting to slap him, after feeling his isolation, I also suffer from a profound need to ease his pain.

I want to hate him. But like Jaxx keeps reminding me, I'm looking at things from a human mindset. Maybe wildlings don't hold grudges against their mates.

"I guess now both of us are unreachable by phone."

Hawk falls silent and stills, staring at my reflection in the glass of a picture hanging on the back wall of the room. "I'm glad Jaxx is feeling better," he says, his voice controlled. "And that you two smoothed out your differences."

*Right*, he smells Jaxx on me.

"That's good," he says, still staring at the back wall. "I'm happy for you."

"You don't seem happy."

He lifts a shoulder. "Maybe I don't know how to be."

"Maybe you don't deserve to be."

He turns and straightens papers on the top of the desk. "I deserve that."

"And more."

He dips his chin but doesn't meet my gaze.

I stare at my self-assured, king of the world and see the truth I suspected. It hurt him to hurt me. It doesn't excuse his actions, but it helps. "You said it takes one to know one. Do you believe that?"

"I do."

I step into the office, close the door, and set my workout clothes on a table inside the door. When his gaze finally rises to mine, I hold out my arms and give him a runway turn as I step closer.

His eyes widen as he takes in the flowing skirt and the way my breasts swell at the neckline. "You have wonderful taste. I bet the people I met today never even guessed I'm nothing but a thieving street-rat whore."

His face tightens, his gaze locked down. "I'm sorry."

The words are gruff and clipped. He isn't the kind of man to apologize. His chiseled jaw flexes and I recognize what it costs him. Good. It's time the billionaire paid some dues.

In the center of the office, I stop and wait until I have his full attention. "I've had sex with eight men in my life and of those, one is Jaxx. Does that make me promiscuous in your eyes? You, the self-proclaimed man-whore who bathes in women, consuming them like ambrosia."

Hawk pegs me with a glare so hostile, I can't tell if it's directed at himself, me, or something else entirely. I have no idea what he's thinking. He hides his thoughts and feelings so well. "I apologized. What more would you have me say?"

"You had me investigated."

"You know I did."

"Let's leave the past in the past and look at who I am now. Did your people find that I live off sugar daddies or con people or manipulate the system to rise to the top?"

"No."

"No," I repeat, jutting my chin. "My bank account has fewer zeros than yours, and maybe I made some choices I regret but I pulled myself up from nothing the same as you. You got further, so what? I don't want your money. This isn't a Cinderella story for me and you're far from Prince Charming. Contact your lawyers and write up whatever prenup, non-disclosure, property agreement takes me out of your finances. I do fine on my own. I won't give you an excuse to question my motives."

Hawk's nostrils flare. "I never thought—"

"Sure, you did. You said as much. It's the way men like you always think. Who cares about money?"

He chuffs. "Most people."

"Well, I don't. Never have. Never will. I care about people. Despite what you said, you won't lose your life's work because of me. I promise you that."

He sticks his fists deep into the pockets of his slacks. "This isn't what I want."

"Clearly. I'm sorry you're here against your will." I point to a spot on the area rug in front of me. "Come here."

"Why?"

"Because I told you to." I wait, wondering if he'll give me the power to tell him what to do.

He locks in and I see him debating his moves. Eventually, though, eyes hooded, he stalks around the desk. Hawk moves like the predator he is and stops right in front of me.

Damn, he smells good. This close, demand rushes over me and my heart beats faster. Despite him being cocky and brusque and broody, I'm not immune to the clit-throbbing draw of the wounded bad boy.

Hawk is more than that, though. He's also vicious and a loner and an autocratic control freak. What demons haunt the soul of the man in front of me?

"You want nothing to do with me. I accept that."

His eyes narrow and I raise my hand to stop him interrupting to deny it.

"You're entitled to your opinion, but you're wrong. I'm *not* a mistake and you being here isn't a mistake, either. I'll pull this quint together and prove that, but you have to give me a goddamn minute to get my bearings."

"You don't—"

I shake my head. "I know what I am and what I'm not better than you. The others agreed that our life together started at the side of the road with my resurrection. I want that for all of us. We are meant to be a unit of five. I can't and won't stop you from going to the Elder Council, but while you are part of this bonding, you'll act like it—until you're not."

Suspicion blankets his expression. "After what I said, you should want me out of your lives like the others do."

I rub my arms, the heat of betrayal rising inside me once again. "Part of me wants to retaliate—but a bigger part of me believes you are in this bonding for a reason and we need to get past this."

"That's ridiculously idealistic."

"Maybe. Seeing how I was murdered this week and

came back to find a new life and new destiny, maybe I'm feeling optimistic. We need to settle this and leave it behind us."

"And how do you suggest—"

My palm hits his cheek with a slap strong enough to spin his head to the side. His neck pivots and it's like he's an owl and not a hawk. He stretches his neck side to side, his steel-gray gaze flaring.

"A good start." I shake my hand and smile. "I get why you said the things you did about me. Do something like that again and you're gone. I don't give a shit about fae magic. If you splay me open a second time, you can live and die alone and sexually forgotten for all I care."

I flex my stinging fingers and peg him with a glare. "You might rule the world, but you don't rule me. You don't get to treat me like a money-grubbing whore."

His guard is down, and I see the hurt boy behind the façade of the powerful man. Regret and sorrow burn in his expression. He's fighting his demons just like me.

I stride over, pick up my workout clothes and head out. I pause with my hand on the door handle and look over my shoulder. "I get that you don't want this mating—that you don't want *me*. If you're determined to get out of this bonding, I won't fight you—not because I don't think we could be great—but because no one should have their choice stripped from them. I wouldn't wish that on my greatest enemy."

"We're not enemies, Calli," he snaps. "I never said that, and I don't feel that way."

"Well, you made it clear we're not friends." I open the door but before I can leave, Hawk throws up his hand. The door pulls out of my grip and slams shut.

He lets off a soft curse and storms forward. "There's something you need to understand, Calli. I'm not a nice man. If you accept that now, it will save a great deal of time and effort. There isn't a gentler, romantic version of man inside me waiting to be coaxed out. I am acerbic. I can be cruel. It's who I am. I'm neither proud of it, nor ashamed. It simply is."

With his dress shirt rolled to his elbows, and his black vest buttoned closed, Hawk gives off a vibe of cool power. The look he pierces me with is equally cold. "It's not something I chose. As your past forged you into the female you are, my past forged me. I can be no other."

The hopelessness in his voice saddens me. I struggle with my feelings. Part of me wants Hawk to accept the possibility of our quint and trust me enough to let his guard down. The other part of me thinks he deserves to have his say and try to win his freedom.

"About severing yourself from our quint…" I say. "I'll support whatever you decide, regardless of my personal feelings. I'll go with you to speak to the elders and make the others understand. There won't be any backlash on you."

Hawk looks no happier than he did when I arrived, but I try not to let it bother me. "Me stepping back is best for everyone. You see that, right?"

"No. That's not at all what I see. The others are going to train me for a few hours outside. You're welcome to join us. I hope you do."

*Brant*

The three of us change quickly and get out of Dodge so Calli can have her say with Hawk without an audience. I want to stay close by in case she needs us, but I'm outvoted by Jaxx and the kid.

"She's strong, Bear, and getting stronger every day," Jaxx says, stretching out his shoulder in the back yard. He swings his arms back and works on the other one. "Let her fight her own battles when she can so she retains a modicum of control."

I know he's right. Still, it goes against every instinct I possess to leave her vulnerable to Hawk after he hurt her.

Kotah shifts into his wolf and trots toward the gate to our private yard. I jog over and let him out. "See you in a few."

Jaxx is done his upper body and has one foot up on the side of the hot tub stretching out his quads and hams. He catches me staring. "Somethin' on your mind, Bear?"

It's the first time since Calli woke up that Jaxx and I have a moment alone together. I've been testing our emotional bond to get a read on him over the past couple of days, and I genuinely like and trust the guy. Checking that the sliding glass door to the great room is closed, I step closer. "You know I'm a first-tier FCO enforcer, yeah?"

Jaxx switches legs and grabs the toe of his shoe, leaning forehead to knee. "Yeah."

"Well, before this guardian situation started, I was working on getting into the investigations unit. I started paying closer attention to the details of my past cases.

You know, honing my investigative skills."

"And?"

"I discovered a swath of duplicity and cover-up going on at high levels of the organization."

Jaxx abruptly stops stretching, checks our surroundings and steps closer. "Be careful sayin' shit like that. You might be the size of a tank but you're not indestructible."

"Oh, I know. And I haven't brought up what I found to anyone before now. Just you."

His brow tightens. "Okay. Why me? Why now? What kind of cover-up are we talkin' about?"

I draw a deep breath. This could go very badly for me, but I gotta believe that if we're to be mates, Jaxx is one of the good guys. "It started with the stuff I would've missed if I hadn't been paying attention."

"For example?"

"Last fall, I took down a troll kid with a wicked strong command of magnetics. He brought a football goal post down on his bully at school. He had a rough transition, so I followed up a few months later."

"And?"

"And his parents had no idea who I was asking about. They invited me in and there wasn't one picture of the kid or any evidence they ever had a kid."

"You sure you got it right?"

"Yeah. After I intervened at the school and released him to the Transitions Unit, I sat on the parents' couch and explained how the boy's evaluation and holding would work. And then, five months later, same parents, same couch, no kid. They were completely wiped."

Jaxx scuffs a rough hand over his mouth. "And you think FCO had somethin' to do with it?"

"Yeah. I looked through my case file at the agency and my notes were altered. There was no record of the kid."

"So how can you be sure—"

"Because I keep a personal log of all my shifts at home and the info was there."

Jaxx curses and his cat lets off a low growl. "Keepin' unapproved records in an unsecured location is a major no-no, Bear. You can do jail time for that."

I shrug. "Do you want to lecture me on protocol or hear about the two other blips I found?"

He throws up his hands. "Yeah, go ahead."

"Also MIA are a sixteen-year-old selkie female who commands water, and a male fairy sapling who generates energy fields. I followed up on both and there's no trace of them—no pictures, no school records, nothing."

Jaxx stares at the cabin a scowl marring his Hollywood hunk beauty. "Pullin' kids with exceptional gifts out of society could be an effort to manage their powers and reduce exposure risks. Maybe they'll be reintegrated into society when they're better equipped."

"Then why wipe them off the map? Why wipe their parents so they don't even remember having kids?"

"Because someone wants to be the only one who knows they exist. They want to harness them under total control." Jaxx is a sharp and strategic guy. Despite not being sure I should open this can of mutiny, he doesn't disappoint.

"Exactly."

"How far up in FCO do you think this goes?"

"Right to the top," I say.

"Okay, I hate where you're headed with this."

I shrug. "Think about it. A guy arrogant enough to go by the moniker, Black Knight, has the clearance and passwords to access confidential FCO files as well as the money and power to extract them, erase their identities, move them, train them and house them somewhere off the grid without people questioning where the orders are coming from. Anyone fitting that description come to mind?"

Jaxx scowls at the office window and I see by his expression that he understands why I don't trust Hawk or want him anywhere near Calli. "*Frickety-frack*."

"Exactly."

# CHAPTER FIFTEEN

*Calli*

After speaking with Hawk, I pee, change, and head out to the fenced-in yard at the back of the cabin. When I slide open the glass door, Jaxx and Brant jump away from each other like I caught them in the act of planning something. "Well, that's not suspicious at all," I say, laughing at their guilty faces. I narrow my gaze on Jaxx. "Was that about me?"

Jaxx looks genuinely shocked. "No, kitten. I'm not one to kiss and tell. We were talkin' FCO business."

"Oh, right, I forgot you work for the same company."

"Hawk's company, actually. Did you know that?"

"No. You work for him?"

"No," Brant snaps, heading to the closed wooden gate. "Hawk happens to be at the helm of an international corporation but we each work for different divisions. I'm in the policing force as an enforcer and Jaxx is an incident first responder. He responds to EMS calls and handles potential exposure due to injury or medical need."

Right. I knew that, though I hadn't put the pieces together. "And Kotah is a university scholar."

My chocolate and silver wolf trots in the gate, his tongue lolling to the side in a whimsical smile. He gives Brant a nod and then the bear turns to me. "All clear. Kotah ran the jogging path and says we're good to start with a run."

"Can you shift back for a sec, Kotah, please?" I ask. "I want to talk with the three of you about Hawk first."

At the mention of our fifth, the teasing comradery evaporates, and their smiles fall. The tension between the guys makes my insides twist. Even Kotah's good mood is no longer apparent as he straightens before me as a young man.

I wonder about leaving it until later, but no. If we intend on standing up at the front of a dinner reception this evening, we need to nip this now.

"What's the matter, beautiful," Brant asks, sniffing the air, his muscles twitching. "Did the avian upset you again?"

I wave that away. "Nothing like that. Look. I get that Hawk isn't an easy fit with your personalities and that he's *acerbic*, as he puts it, but I want you to cut him some slack and let him find his way in this bonding."

Brant growls. "You're too kindhearted. He doesn't deserve your forgiveness after what he said about you."

I cross my arms over my chest. "I nearly killed Jaxx and he forgave me. It would be hypocritical to not offer Hawk a chance to make things right."

"You never meant to hurt Jaxx like you did," Brant says. "Hawk's intention was to hurt you."

"The point is that he said things about *me*. If I want to make peace, that should carry the most weight."

The three of them look as if they think my logic is flawed. It doesn't matter. "I'm the phoenix in this bonding, and I understand why he did what he did. He knew I'd never break down without being torn down. He saved Jaxx's life as much or more than my tears did. Give him a pass or a wide berth, but either way, he gets a chance to right his wrongs."

Kotah exhales heavily. "And you're certain that's what you want?"

The breeze catches my hair and I pull it away from my face. "Yes. I haven't had a home or a family I can count on in more than a decade. If we're doing this, we're finding our way together. No man is left behind."

Jaxx dips his chin and nods. "As you wish. Hawk gets a pass. If he makes an effort, I will meet him halfway."

Kotah nods. "Agreed."

Brant is the one holding out, and the one I know hates this idea the most. He elevated himself to my guardian of both body and heart from the very beginning.

"What do you say, big guy?"

"I say there's a lot we don't know about him. You can't take someone like that at face value. He's cunning and dark."

"There is a lot the five of us don't know about one another. Layers of past experience and wounds and upbringing change how people interact." I close the distance between us and take Brant's hand. "Please,

Bear. Trust me. I'm a big girl and I want us to try."

Brant growls again, but it's more a grumbly sound of letting out his frustration. Once he falls silent, he wraps a heavy arm around my shoulder and kisses the top of my head. "How do I deny you anything?"

I reach up to kiss the bottom of his jaw and brush a thumb over the day's growth. "You don't. Thank you. It'll be fine, you'll see. Now, did someone say something about warming up with a run?"

*Kotah*

Sitting cross-legged on the grass opposite Calli, I position her close enough that our knees touch. I massage her hands where they fall in the shared space in front of our laps and swing them to ensure she is loose and relaxed. Our run went well, Brant evaluated her balance and strength, and Jaxx went over a few basic self-defense moves—most of which she was familiar with. Now, it's my turn to work on inner strength.

"Close your eyes and focus on your breathing. In. Out. On the in, fill your lungs all the way to the floor of your pelvis. On the out, push all the worry and stress up your throat and force it out of your body."

I breathe with her, working to help her find her center. In truth, even after an intimate morning with Jaxx, she's back to being tightly strung and anxious. She's like a coiled spring about to snap. Potential energy building to explode.

"Now, we're going to visualize. On your inward breath, pick something that's upsetting you. Focus on it. Give it an image in your mind. Then, on the outward breath speak the name in one word and set it free. Understand?"

She nods, focused, and attentive.

"Breathe in and picture it… now exhale and name it."

Her breasts rise as her lungs fill and as her lips open on the exhale, she speaks her truth. "Riley."

"Good. Now take a few more breaths and search your soul for the next stressor you need to release. On the intake, visualize. On the exhale, name it and release it. There's no wrong answer and I'll never question you or judge you on anything we share. You're safe here, Calli."

She draws two more breaths before she says, "Hawk."

A moment later, she says, "Aroused."

And then, "Vulnerable."

And, "Broken."

With that, her shoulders relax, her breathing slows. She's finished exhuming her worries and frustrations. Keeping my voice quiet, I think about the sensations my body experiences as I connect with my wolf.

"With your eyes still closed, open yourself up to the power that now lives within you. Maybe it's a glow you feel in your chest or a spark in your fingers or an ache in your bones of the promise of power. Whatever it is, connect with it now and greet it with welcome."

She breathes in and out for a few more breaths and frowns. Her fingers tighten in mine. "I'm trying. I feel it, but it doesn't want to come to me."

I can't imagine having the kind of power Calli does

and not being able to connect with it. It must course through her cells in chaos. "Don't worry. Stay relaxed. Stay focused. You're not trying to call your phoenix. You merely want to make friends with the power behind her. Immerse yourself in the sensation of the energy."

She dips her chin and continues with her breathing.

"No expectations, Calli. Just a meet and greet."

After a couple of more breaths, I know she's getting there. Her fingers warm in mine and her skin starts to glow.

She's breathtaking.

"That power is part of you now. Welcome it into your soul. Accept it unconditionally. It is here to help you grow into the female you are meant to become."

I feel the tingle of her magic in our joined hands. It speaks to my wolf, and calls my animal side forward. When a tear rolls down her cheek, I cup her face and catch it with a gentle sweep of my thumb.

"You're doing amazing, Calli. I'm so proud of you."

Her eyes open and the emerald green is ringed by the dancing flames of her phoenix. A fiery second color that is both entrancing and slightly unnerving.

This is who Calli was reborn to become. My mate.

The hunger I felt in the backseat of Hawk's truck overtakes me as my wolf ascends. With my hand cupping her cheek, I tug her closer, lean forward, and kiss her.

She groans, tilting her head, and sealing her mouth to mine. Her soft lips are firm, the gentleness I exert soon abandoned to the pressure she desires. I sigh as her tongue slips inside my mouth, tasting me in long, leisurely licks.

Calli's kiss is confident, skilled, and laced with enough aggression to bring my wolf howling to the foreground. In another second, I'm flat on my back and she's pressed full-body on top of me. I'm achingly aware of her needs, her arousal driving me wild. Except…

I growl as reality sets in. I ease back and try to calm my wolf. "We need to move inside, *Chigua*. This isn't the place."

Calli groans and I hate myself even more for breaking the moment. I'm aroused, my urge to mate pounding hard in my veins, yet my duty as her guardian overrules everything. "The Bastion is a place of rules, politics, and expectations. We should keep our private lives private."

"I saw people this morning and I didn't judge."

"Yes, but the eyes of the fae people are on us. Expectations are being formed."

She rolls off my hips and flops back onto the grass, heaving for breath. "I'm sorry. You're right… gawd, I can't get a handle on my hunger for you guys. I'm not this sexually depraved."

I stand, turn to adjust things in my pants, and then offer her a hand to lift her off the grass. "No judgment. Besides, I started it. You're incredibly beautiful… and this mating heat is consuming… and I'm so honored you're mine."

When we get to the glass doors, she pulls me against her body and runs her hand down the back of my jogging pants. Her grip on my backside speaks to how out of control we both still feel. "Consider that foreplay.

Tonight, after the reception, I want to strip you down, and have my way with you."

I let off a long low growl. "I'll count the minutes."

*Hawk*

"Fine. Take these. What else did she send?"

Lukas accepts the folder of signed files and pauses, as if unsure whether to speak.

"*What?*"

"You're not all right, so I won't ask if you are. Is there anything I can do?"

"I'm fine," I lie. The truth is, my cheek is still on fire, courtesy of the smack of justice served to me by my phoenix a few hours ago. I work my jaw from side to side. Between Brant's fist the other day and Calli's slap, a few teeth are loose. That isn't where my discomfort stems from though.

My cock aches. My head pounds. My life was yanked from my control, *annnd* worse than all that times a million—another male marked my mate.

I stare at the letter opener at the top of the desk and eat the burn of sexual frustration. Having Calli stand before me with the jaguar's scent of sex on her skin…

I close my eyes and breathe through my hawk's rage.

My talons pierce my nailbeds for the hundredth time and I want to scream. Calli took Jaxx into her body.

To say it doesn't trigger every ounce of my violent, competitive nature, would be a lie. A big one. In all things, I must be the best, the first, the greatest, the most.

It serves me well in life. It doesn't serve me well in this mating.

Ruthless won't work with Calli. There is, unquestionably a social usefulness to being polite, and treading lightly around other peoples' sensitivities.

I don't inherently possess that trait. Why do I care?

"Sir?"

*Right.* He asked me a question. "I'm fine. What's next?"

Without questioning the obvious stench of my lie in the air, he hands me a tablet queued up on a news story about a trucker's remains found burned in Texas. "The human authorities don't know what to make of it. They can't explain what could've burned so hot out in a clearing like that."

"There's nothing to tie Calli to this?"

He shakes his head. "The only one who saw her jump in the cab of his semi once he left the diner is you."

Good. The asshole deserved to fry. I tap the tablet and scroll through my emails. Almost two hundred a day and I care about maybe ten. I start responding to those. "Is everything ready for tonight for the others?"

"The wardrobes were set out this afternoon. I've spoken with the caterers and had shellfish removed from the menu on Kotah's behalf. The felines weren't pleased, but it's taken care of. You and Jaxx will sit to either side of your phoenix, then the wolf next to you and the bear next to the jaguar."

"And the introduction?"

"Gareth is acting as Master of Ceremonies. He read

over what you prepared and agreed to use it."

"Good. Pomp and fawning will only serve to make her uneasy in a situation that is bound to overwhelm. A simple introduction is best." I sign off the tablet and hand it back. "And the response from my meeting with the elders?"

"I'll let you know as soon as I hear."

"The sooner the better." I yawn and scrub a rough hand over my face. Between staying on top of FCO management, anticipating the public response for the arrival of a phoenix, worrying about Calli's safety after the ambush, and this insane mating heat pounding in my cock, sleep has escaped me all week. I shake my head and push up to my feet. "Give me twenty minutes to shower and dress for dinner. We'll head to the reception as a group."

## CHAPTER SIXTEEN

*Calli*

When I step around the stone wall of the fireplace, I'm wondering if my girls might burst from the bodice of the ice-blue gown I'm wearing. Hawk has such elegant taste, but I worry this dress highlights how far I'm reaching instead of who I am. It's stunning—that's not the issue—it's just…

I cast a glance across the great room and my mind fractures. My breath lodges in my throat and they catch me standing there with my mouth hanging open.

"You guys are… wow."

Jaxx and Brant sit, reclining in traditional tuxedos, Kotah is wearing dark chestnut hide pants, a ceremonial beaded jacket, and a silver wolf claw over his choker, and Hawk, off in the back, is dark and dangerous in all black. No, not *all* black, on his jacket, he wears a tiny gold lapel pin of a phoenix, it's wings back and flaming.

Wow. How can I even see it, let alone detect the intricate design? Now that I'm looking for it, they all have one. "Guys, honestly… you four… there aren't words. My heart aches."

Brant rises from the arm of one of the sofas and

kisses my hand. "And yet we pale in your radiance." He wraps his strong arms around me and gives me a slow, dancefloor spin. "You'll blow the doors of the place tonight."

Kotah stands and waits for Brant to nod and step back. My wolf comes to me, offering up a black gift box nestled in his palm. "For you, my *Chigua*."

I accept the box and smile. "You've called me that before. What does it mean?"

"In my family tongue, *Chigua* means greatly beloved war woman. It is a title of honor for a woman who exhibits true heroism on the battlefield."

"I haven't earned such high praise, yet."

He doesn't seem to agree. "Your entire life has been a battle to retain your grace in the face of hardship. You are a warrior, Calli, and I am proud to be one of your guardians."

My sweet wolf. I kiss his cheek and then open the box.

Under layers of gold tissue, I find a leather charm bracelet intricately woven into a leather cuff. I lift it from its wrapping and examine the five, tiny wooden animal carvings bound within the intertwining strands. I brush the pad of my finger over the depictions of each of us and lose sight of them behind a wall of moisture blocking my vision.

"Thank you," I say, my voice choked. I hold it out to him to tie it on. "Will you?"

Kotah wraps the leather ends around my wrist several times and knots the bracelet on my wrist. "I thought the wider band of a cuff would fair better than something more feminine and delicate. We seem to find ourselves in unexpected situations and I can't see that changing anytime soon."

"I'm not that feminine and delicate myself. It's perfect."

"You really like it?"

"I'll never take it off." I cup his face in my hands and kiss him. I love his gift and appreciate the time he took in crafting it. As always, my best intentions fly out the window once I connect with him.

Kotah is more comfortable with me in his arms each time I end up here. His calming nature and youthful passion are addictive. It's not the sharp, lusty pull I feel when I'm near Jaxx. It's sweeter. He's warm chocolate melting on my tongue.

I can't get enough of him.

A male chuckle rumbles beside us and I remember the others are watching and waiting. "I think that's a yes, pup. I'd say she likes it very much."

I ease back, breathless and meet Brant's playful gaze. "Hello, Bear."

Brant winks. "Hello to you, beautiful."

I turn to Kotah, standing at my side and finger his silky hair. He's wearing it down tonight and it makes him look exotic. "Thank you. Your gift is beautiful and thoughtful, and it fills my heart that you crafted it for me. Yes, I love it."

Kotah's smile is as sweet as it is genuine.

My world recalibrates as things I didn't understand shift into place within me. When I look deep into Brant's golden eyes, certainties resonate in my soul. The four of us were strangers only days ago, but now we're not.

They are mine… or at least, they can be.

Brant's waiting patiently, as always. He's never pushed in or tried to advance on me, instead, he watches over me and protects me without expecting anything in return.

I rake my fingers through his dark hair and love how it hangs in loose, messy waves to his broad shoulders. "It occurs to me that you and I haven't had much time together, Bear."

He slides a strong arm around my back and pulls us chest to chest. "Good thing I'm in this for the long term."

I reach up on my tiptoes but still come nowhere close to his lips. Strong hands against my ribs lift me so I see him eye to eye. I wet my lips with my tongue, consumed by the hopeful anticipation beaming in his expression.

"What do you say, Bear? Care to try out our chemistry?"

"Thought you'd never ask." He pulls me close and I close the distance to his mouth. Whatever this is, the wildling mating bond or a phoenix and her guardian thing or the devotion of a male who seems to genuinely care about me, it is bliss to kiss him. Magic.

Where a kiss with Kotah is reverence and excitement, Brant's is confident and filled with promises. As his mouth claims mine, the primal growl of his bear rumbles in my chest and my nipples tighten under the smooshed bodice of my gown. I follow the primal call, deepening the kiss, gripping a fistful of hair as his tongue's teasing caress invades. The man has a gift. One

I'm now hungry to explore.

Is this what it will be like? Sweet mercies, I hope so.

After what feels like an age, but couldn't have been much more than a few minutes, a gentle hand presses on my back. "Kitten, as much as I wish we could stay in together tonight and explore our bond. We are expected."

*Right.* I recede from the sexual spell Kotah and then Brant put me under and end our kiss. "That was lovely, Bear. Hold that thought."

"Consider it an open invitation."

When my feet touch the ground, my legs aren't strong enough to hold me steady. Jaxx takes possession of me then. His wide, white smile dazzles me and I recognize the intent in his turquoise eyes. "I thought you said, we need to leave?"

"Your longings must wait until later, but fair is fair. If they get to say how delectable you look in this dress and give you a good luck kiss for tonight, then so do I."

Over the hours shared this morning, Jaxx and I grew comfortable with one another. Not only comfortable but possessive. His fingers press on the nape of my neck and pull me into his kiss. My hand slides down the front of his pants and I rub the heel of my palm over the hard ridge filling out the front of his suit pants.

The purr that rips from his chest is all sex and seduction. It stirs up images of our naked play this morning and makes me want to strip down and ditch the entire evening outside this cabin.

Jaxx is the one to end the kiss. He checks that I'm steady on my feet and then brushes the back of his finger along my jaw. "Save a dance for me, kitten. I want to show you off."

With my mind spinning, I turn to the back of the room.

Hawk has his spine pressed against the wall beside a mahogany sideboard. He's taking it all in, his posture dominant, his stance tense. I start toward him and focus on my footing. I don't want to faceplant on the floor before I close the distance. As I draw nearer, he eyes me warily.

But as guarded as he is, hunger smolders in his gaze.

Our bond is strengthening. We all feel the same pull. I feel how much he wants me, despite himself. Yes, I'm still hurt and angry, but I meant what I said to the others this afternoon. Jaxx forgave me. I will work on forgiving Hawk.

I stop right before him and hold out my hand. "What do you say, Hawk? Before you decide whether or not to walk away, don't you think you should sample the goods and maybe see what it could be like?"

He purses his lips in an arrogant smile and his jaw flexes. "I have no doubt the mating bond makes it seem incredible but that's not reality."

"Reality is merely an illusion," I say, quoting Einstein. I place my hand against the silky lapel of his suit and touch the little phoenix pin. He's behind this. I see his little touches in the details of our lives. They're small things but they prove that we're always on his mind.

"I won't beg," I say. "You know I want you to give this a chance. If you think that even a little kiss is too much for you to commit to, then I support your right to say no."

The challenge in my voice brings the rush of his animal side rising to meet me head on—as I expected. I take a half-step closer and the hair on my arms stands on end.

When I think he might grapple me and press hard against my body, he bends forward and gives me a brusque brush of his lips. "The dress doesn't do you justice, Spitfire. Still, you will outshine every female there with the glory of a radiant sun next to the short-lived light of shooting stars."

I barely got a taste of him and my heart beats faster with the threat that he'll let this moment slip away from us. "Come now, Hawk. Are you afraid I'll ruffle your feathers? Kiss me, like you mean it. Show me what all the fuss is about. You bathe in women, right? Show me the magic."

His steel-gray eyes narrow on me as a hungry sound reverberates from his chest. Nope. He has himself locked down so tight, he's not going to do anything he doesn't want to.

I am going to lose him.

*Hawk*

*Fuck me.* The pleading panic in Calli's eyes cuts me to the core of my dark soul. How can she want me anywhere near her when she's seen what I am? I said she's not good enough for me but it's the other way around. After the things I've said and done, I am the blight on this mating.

"Okay, Hawk," she says, taking a step back. "Keeping it simple is probably a good idea."

The acidic aroma of the lie mixes with the tang of her disappointment. I curse myself. I swore I'd never intentionally hurt her again and I turn around and reject her in front of the others, right before she's set to face the fae leaders.

*Fuck. Fuck. Fuck.* This is going to bite me in the ass.

Without consideration of the price I'll pay, I catch her wrist and yank her back. She comes so willingly it cleaves a chink in my armor. She's too fucking trusting. I turn her in my arms, pinning her against the wall, so I don't have to think about the other three watching us.

This is for Calli and only her.

I grip her head and tip it back, in a lavish, heated meeting of our mouths. Calli's kiss is passionate and demanding. She's greedy and I wish rising to that call is in the cards for us. It's not. Still, if this is my one moment to claim those lush full lips, I won't waste it.

Kissing Calli is everything I feared—and more.

Her need speaks to me at a level I can't control. She's scorching hot and hungry—but that's on the surface. Beneath her wanton, connected like this, her soul seeks mine, needing something from me she doesn't get from the others.

There's a darkness inside her she's afraid to let them see. For the first time in a week, it occurs to me that something more than money and position placed me on the guardian roster. I understand hiding the darkness within.

Maybe we're not a total cosmic mistake.

My body settles as my hawk stands down. Is this the contact my animal side is craving? It's not even a need to fuck her—it's the need to find her, to acknowledge her.

Buried somewhere behind the barriers brought on by years of deflection and survival, she forced part of herself into hiding. My beaten and abused soul recognizes a fellow victim.

Not that either of us is a victim now.

"Earth to Hawk," Brant says, over my shoulder. "We all get the addiction, but *tick-tock* bigshot."

It takes a moment for my mind to catch up with my soul. Calliope Tannis is nothing I would've chosen for myself.

And yet here she is.

"Right. Sorry."

Calli sways as I step back and release her. She presses a hand flat on the wall for support. "Don't be sorry. Not for getting swept away kissing me like that."

I check my watch. "Shit. We need to go."

I turn, intending to allow one of the others the honor of escorting Calli arm-in-arm, except, she slides her hand around my elbow and meets my stride.

*Damn*. I knew this would bite me in the ass.

*Calli*

My brain is mush and my knees are weak. It's a good thing Hawk is holding me up on one side and Jaxx on the other. What I feel for each of them is different yet essential to the whole. It's hard to wrap my head around that, but I understand more with each passing moment I spend with them.

And yeah, *wow*. I'm more than a little light-headed.

"You're far more relaxed than I thought you'd be," Kotah says, smiling as we break the line of trees into the clearing near the main lodge.

"I learned to meditate this afternoon."

Hawk chuffs. "I watched your session from the office window. The young wolf seems to confuse the concepts of meditation with making out."

My cheeks flush warm at the memory. "No complaints here. And hey, it eased a lot of my stresses."

"The mark of success," Brant adds, laughter in his voice.

*This*. This is what our bond is supposed to feel like. I smile and press my cheek to Hawk's shoulder. "I told you I'd pull it together. I can do this, Hawk. *We* can do this. Don't give up on me before I get a chance to prove it."

Hawk shakes his head and frowns at me. "I grew up around a lot of four-letter words, Spitfire. Love was never one of them. Don't waste your heart on me. You're getting swept away by a kiss. It was only that—a kiss."

I roll my eyes. "A great kiss. A panty-dampening, mind-altering, blow your load kind of kiss."

Hawk arches a brow. "Perhaps you should get your mind off seminal emissions and into the night ahead. The Fae Council runs our world. First impressions and all that."

I wink at him and smile. "Nice deflection."

*Jaxx*

I'm not sure it's a good thing that Calli's determined to bring Hawk into the fold. She feels the pull of the mating bond, but the level of emotion driving that is overwhelming. If Brant's right and our FCO corporate kingpin is amassing an army of exceptional fae, things won't go well for us when the shit hits. I hate the idea of conspiring with Brant and investigating him but can't abide standing by if what the bear suspects is true.

Accepting Hawk into our mated life must be approached in slow degrees… assuming he changes his mind and sticks around. If he severs himself from our bond—which I doubt is even possible—it might be the best solution all around.

Having arrived later than expected, the ballroom below is filled to bursting when we stop on the mezzanine overlooking the reception. The event is open to all species but thankfully, due to the short notice, there isn't more than two or three hundred attendees.

My cat prowls forward and I sniff the air. How can… Where are they? There. My gaze locks on a dapper couple standing at a table in the center of the room.

Mama's face lights up like Times Square when she sees me. Daddy straightens beside her, his proud smile firmly locked in place. "And that's why they didn't answer the phone this morning."

Calli glances over at me and then follows my gaze.

"The blond woman in the royal blue dress and the man at her side." When Calli's gaze finds them, Mama gives her a wave and blows us both a kiss.

Calli looks from them to me and then pales. "Your parents are *here?* They flew here to meet me?"

The way her high pitched panic leaks out is too cute. I pull her to my side and kiss the side of her face. "Relax, kitten. This is our night. They just want to share in it."

A mountain elf named Gareth finishes checking in with Hawk and lifts the mic to his mouth. "Everyone, our guests of honor have arrived. May I introduce to you Calliope Tannis, our newly resurrected phoenix, and her guardians, Sir Hawk Barron, Jaxx Stanton, Brantley Robbins, and His Royal Highness, Prince Nakotah Northwood, heir to the Fae Prime."

The sea of guests below breaks into a wide-eyed round of curtsies and head bobs. The collective gasp doesn't only hiss out of their lips. Calli and I rubberneck it past Hawk and look at Kotah while Brant mutters, "What the fuck?" far too loudly for such a formal setting.

Kotah looks mortified.

"Later," Hawk hisses, recovering quickly and smiling out at the masses. "Everyone, wave at the nice people."

We follow Hawk's instruction and are almost blinded by the photo flashes that follow. The Royal Prince? Seriously?

Gareth gestures for us to head down the carpeted steps to start through a reception line. People begin stepping away from their tables in a rush to get in line.

My gaze darts over Calli's face, and my insides melt. My longing to protect her is so acute, it physically hurts. The spice of char in her scent is stronger than usual, and I pray she doesn't panic and fry the king of one of the more violent races. "We've got you, kitten. Relax. No need to flame up."

She blinks up at me, her emotions guarded.

"Deep, cleansing breaths," Kotah says, coming at her from the other side. He runs a gentle caress up her bare arm. Thankfully, easing her seems to ease his own distress of being outed. "You're not alone, *Chigua*. Your guardians are here with you."

"Pain with a purpose," Hawk whispers quietly enough so that only we four hear. "Once we get through this, we can get some answers. Chin up. Eyes bright."

Lukas waits at the bottom of the stairs and escorts us through the handshakes. Hawk takes the lead. He knows many of the faces and introduces us as a group. Touching the Prime Prince is a social sin, so Kotah is free to keep Calli's hand linked with his. Brant and I take the back of the pack.

We meet up with my parents close to the end and I take the lead on the meet and greet. "Everyone, these are my parents, Jonathan and Magdalene Stanton. Mama, Daddy, this is Calli, Kotah, Brant, and Hawk."

Despite Calli's fears, their first meeting goes exactly as I knew it would. Mama hugs all around. Daddy kisses Calli's cheek, stunned by her beauty, and says how honored they are to welcome her and the guys to our family pride.

"In one week," Daddy says, "we gained three sons and a daughter. That's a blessing beyond measure. We can't wait to get to know you all better."

When we finish the procession, Lukas escorts us to

the head table, so we can be put on display.

Awesome. There's nothing like three-hundred of the most powerful and influential people of the fae world staring at you while you slurp your soup.

"So, kid," Brant says, leaning behind me to talk to Kotah at the other end of the table. "Maybe being the crowned prince to our world is something you mention to people you're supposed to share a life with. Just saying."

"I'm sorry," Kotah says. "I never meant to deceive you."

Calli takes a few gulps of her bubbly and shrugs. "It's okay. You would've told us when you were ready."

Brant laughs. "The best part is that Sir Barron is no longer top dog. Suck it, Hawk. Bow down to the prince."

Hawk shoots Brant the finger under the table so no one else can see. I can't help but laugh.

"If you'll excuse me a moment." Kotah removes his napkin from his lap and pushes back from the table.

Calli's right on his heels. Hawk curses and follows them out. That leaves Brant and I sitting by our lonesome at our end of the table.

"So much for our first evenin' out."

Brant flicks his hand at the waiter, and he brings over a tray of champagne. We each grab a couple of flutes and drink deep. "This is going to be one hell of a night."

# CHAPTER SEVENTEEN

*Kotah*

"Kotah, wait up." I stop outside the ballroom doors and let Calli catch up. Jogging in heels isn't one of her life skills and I don't want her to break her neck on the night when all eyes are on us. She takes my hand and steps around to face me and—"Oh, gawd, sweetie. It's not that bad is it?"

The utter devastation of my world? It is that bad, yes.

She casts a glance around and pulls me into the ladies' washroom.

"Calli, wait, I can't…"

"Fancy places like this usually have a separate—yep." She pulls me into a private lounge area and locks the door.

"I'm sorry," I say, my voice thick in my throat. "I know I should've said something, but for once… is it wrong to want to keep my private pain private?"

Her breath is warm against my neck as she pulls me against her in a tight hug. A gentle hand strokes down my hair and rests at the small of my back. "If anyone understands wanting to decide what people know about you, it's me. You wanted us to know you based on your own merits. I completely understand and don't blame you at all."

Easing back, I search her expression for any hint that she's being kind. "Truly? You don't mind?"

"Mind that you're a prince or that you'd rather not be? Either way, no, I don't mind. You're my guy." She cups my jaw in her hands and brushes my lips with a kiss. It's amazing how that brief connection helps restore my sense of equilibrium in this new world of ours.

"Kotah, you supported me, protected me, even got shot for me. You took the time to teach me about this world and myself. And you made my beautiful bracelet… That was all you, not some prince prime heir or whatever."

Her hand over my heart brings my wolf forward. "You were already my sweet prince. This just makes it official."

I draw a deep breath and exhale.

"Out with what's upsetting you, right?"

I am so incredibly grateful to the universe for setting me on this course. "And the student surpasses the teacher."

The sound of her laughter resonates within me. "Hardly. I have a feeling you'll be teaching me things for years to come. I'm looking forward to that a great deal."

*So am I.* "Though there are quite a few things I'd like you to teach me tonight after this reception. We made a date to explore our physical relationship. I pray my omission doesn't jeopardize that."

"Aw, sweet wolf, nothing to worry about there. I still want to rip your clothes off and mount you."

Thank the Powers.

There's a knock on the door followed by the *click* of the lock opening and Hawk, Brant, and Jaxx joining us.

Jaxx looks us over. "Everything all right in here?"

"Yep," Calli says, checking with me to ensure that's true.

I turn and lift my hair from the nape of my neck. "Calli, would you remove my pendant and choker, please."

She releases the clasps and I unhook both. When they pull free from my throat, I drop them into the pocket of my doeskin jacket. When I turn to face them, Calli's jaw drops. "Um, wow, that's beautiful."

Beneath the black leather choker, I hid an intricate tattoo of intertwining vines and detailed fretwork. It's penned in a deep wine color with blacks, browns, and greens. The ink has magical fae ingredients that glisten like no other tattoos in the realm. And over the center of my throat sits the royal family crest with a wolf's head tipped back and howling at a full moon.

"Damn, cub," Hawk says, eyeing the artwork. "That's fucking spank."

"Wait a minute," Brant says, frowning as he takes in the room. "Women have couches in their washroom? Men don't get couches. That's hardly fair."

Calli laughs and hugs me, pressing her breast against my chest. "I'm sorry you didn't get to tell us on your terms. That sucks. But it changes nothing. Does it, guys?"

Jaxx and Brant both shake their head but Hawk flashes her a wide-eyed look that implies she's lost her mind.

"What?"

"It's nice that you think so, Spitfire, but having the Prime Prince as one of your guardians *does* change things. It makes some things easier and others much more difficult. There are laws about how he is to be treated, accommodated, where he can reside, who gains access to him. How does he fight at your side when he's supposed to have guards of his own?"

"I don't care about any of that," I say, my heart racing. "I'm one of five. That's all. Please, let it be as simple as that."

Hawk frowns and then Calli's brow furrows as well. "You didn't rat him out, did you? I know you investigated me, but I will be *sooo* pissed if this sideswipe drama has your name on it too—"

"Yes, I investigated all of you," Hawk snaps, showing no remorse as we turn to glare at him. "But I didn't know about our young prince, and I wasn't the one who outed him."

"Then who did?"

"*I did.*" I follow the female voice to the woman standing in the doorway. Petite and regal, she shares the same chestnut hair and tattoo fretwork as me.

There's no mistaking who she is.

"Hello, Mother," I say, forcing down my chaotic feelings, to assume my role as her well-mannered son. I meet her at the doorway and greet her with a kiss to both cheeks. "You are radiant, as always."

"Prima," Hawk says, placing his arm across his middle and bowing. "It's an honor, Your Highness."

"Prima," both Jaxx and Brant say, following suit, bowing and dropping their gazes.

Calli looks lost, so I swoop in, shift her to face my mother, and wrap my arms around her from behind. "Calli, this is my mother, Malayna. Mother, this is Calliope Tannis, our phoenix."

I want to claim her as my mate but bite my tongue. Things are going well between us and I want Calli to be the one to announce her claim on me when she's ready.

"It's a pleasure, Highness," Calli says, her hands trembling under my touch. "Your son is truly an exceptional young man. I would've been lost the past days without him."

I'm not sure if I'm holding Calli up or she's supporting me, but I'm thankful to have my arms wrapped around her. I kiss the side of her neck and breathe in her scent to settle my nerves. "I'm pleased to see you, Mother, don't misunderstand, but why have you come?"

She arches a manicured brow, her smile subtle and reserved. "Your time of hiding in the shadows is at its end Nakotah. You are a Guardian of the Phoenix. No one can challenge your worth now."

*Except Father*. "Does he know you are here?"

Mother frowns and casts a glance at the others.

"It's all right, Mother. I have no secrets from Calli and the others. If we are to be the legendary guardians the fae world needs, we must have faith in our trust for one another."

Mother doesn't look pleased. "I came to bring you home, Nakotah. Your father's time as Prime nears its end. You must return with me and ready to assume leadership."

*Hawk*

The five of us manage to keep up a social front through dinner but skip the dance and retire early after extending our thanks to the dignitaries for a wonderful welcome. Kotah being the imminent Fae Prime changes things. How do we face the challenges demanded of us if he's bound to govern from a royal palace? How do I ensure Calli's safety as our phoenix if I now have to consider enemies out to target Kotah as well?

"Apologies," Kotah says as we head back to the cabin to pack up. "I had no idea that my familial duties would come to play so soon. Father has always seemed invincible and determined that I never take his place."

"That's shitty, kid," Brant says.

"I'm sorry, Kotah," I say, and genuinely mean it. I know the sting of a father's disdain. "Your mother was right to come. We need to get you home to address this."

The spark of hopeful anticipation that lit his eyes an hour ago is gone. It's obvious now that Nakotah is no stranger to judgment yet seems the least cynical of all of us. It will be a true loss if that light is extinguished.

I check my phone as a message vibrates against my hip.

"What is it?" Calli asks. She doesn't miss a thing.

"The Fae Council has called us for an audience. I spoke to them this afternoon and was awaiting—"

"*When* this afternoon," Calli snaps. "Before or after I asked you to give us a chance?"

I scrub a rough hand over my eyes. Will this headache ever lessen? "After, but that has—"

"*Really?* Even after we talked you ran to them to set you free?" The sudden rush of heat explodes from her and her hair blows back like she's a supermodel in front of a fan.

"Cool it, Spitfire," I say, the stir in my slacks becoming a real problem. "This isn't that. This is about your resurrection and our purpose in the days to come."

She clamps her mouth shut and frowns. "Oh."

"Yeah, oh," I say, turning back the way we came. "There is a car waiting for us in the main lot. Sorry, Kotah. Your homecoming will have to wait."

*Calli*

The five of us pile out of the limousine that shuttles us from the lodge over to the Bastion castle. The car ride was quiet. Hawk was broody. Kotah was understandably anxious. Jaxx and Brant kept sharing strange furtive glances. And I worried the half-digested game hen in my stomach might make a sudden attempt at escape.

The night air helps but doesn't quiet the dozens of questions spinning in my head. "What did the historic accounts say about what I'll be called to do when I arrive?"

Kotah slows his step until we're walking side by side toward the massive, gold-embossed doors. "I'm afraid, other than finding a few references to aligning the phoenix and her guardians and uniting the realms, I don't know."

"Aligning us?" Jaxx says. "What does that mean?"

"Apologies. I don't know."

"No need to apologize, sweetie." I collect his hand in mine and lace our fingers. "You can only find what's been put in the books in the first place. If they don't spell it out, we'll have to wait for the big reveal."

"And what do eleven geezers in robes know about us anyway?" Brant asks. "Seems to me if we need aligning, that's for us to figure out, not them."

Hawk says nothing.

The male who meets us in the parking lot is the same male who announced us at the reception—Gareth, I think his name is. He leads us through a polished marble entrance, down a corridor, and into a secured room.

He stops just inside the doorway and points toward a domed pedestal rising from the floor. "Lock any weapons you carry in the bin and step onto the platform when you're ready. Secure the door to ensure your belongings remain untouched."

He stares at me a moment longer than I'm comfortable with and my guys sense it. When they bristle, Gareth drops his gaze and turns to leave. "Good luck to you all."

Brant follows him to the door, and once he's out, activates a high-tech deadbolt and punches a five-digit code into the keypad.

"What's this about?" I ask.

Hawk grabs the handle on the dome cabinet and lifts it open. "The platform to access the council chamber won't rise if it detects weapons. Many powerful people claim an audience with the Fae Council. This antechamber system ensures that no one will catch us unarmed and unaware."

"But we aren't carrying—" My objection stumbles on my tongue as Hawk opens his suit jacket and pulls a gun from both sides of a double shoulder holster. Jaxx's gun is removed from under his tux jacket at the small of his back. Brant takes off what I thought were cufflinks and hands them over. And Kotah unsheathes a wicked-looking knife from his hip.

"What the hell, guys? Were you expecting an ambush between dinner and dancing?"

Brant chuckles and pierces me with a sultry smile. "We're more than your arm candy, beautiful. We're your guardians, remember?"

"I… I guess I figured you were deadly enough with your animal selves. I never thought about packing heat."

Jaxx takes my hand and tugs me onto a round platform. "Oh, our animal selves are deadly, kitten. But, expect the unexpected. Always be prepared, right guys?"

I eye the pile of weapons and shake my head. "You four are so not Boy Scouts."

Hawk and Brant join us on the platform and step directly in front of me. Kotah positions himself on my empty side. Jaxx's arm around my hip tightens as Hawk presses his palm against a control button and we start to rise.

"Relax," Jaxx whispers. "Let's get some answers."

# CHAPTER EIGHTEEN

*Calli*

The Fae Council chamber is set in a semi-circular room with the straight wall at our backs and eleven fae leaders in front of us, seated on a raised platform that arcs from left to right. Behind the dignitaries, a beautiful mural spans the long concave wall, depicting a world and history I never knew existed.

A woman stands in the center and opens her arms to us. She's incredibly tall, with a delicate, willowy frame and a powder pink tinge to her skin. Her eyes are as round as two moons and glisten, reflecting light like iridescent pearls. "Welcome, Calliope. Welcome, gentlemen. Thank you for joining us."

"Minister," Hawk says, bowing his head. "We're honored to oblige the call and eager to learn more about the destiny of the phoenix."

The woman offers him a private smile and my hackles rise. "Who would've guessed this as an outcome. I can't say I'm surprised that the universe chose you to lead the charge, Barron, but it certainly is—"

Hawk steps aside and pulls me to step to the front. "It's Calliope who leads the charge, Minister. She is our queen and is quickly growing into her place as the phoenix she was reborn to be."

A tightening at the side of her glossed lips cinches it. This woman is part of Hawk's 'ambrosia crowd.' The look she gives me drips with derision. "Yet, until a week ago, she wasn't even one of us. She was raised as a mundane nary, is that right? And an unremarkable one at that."

I lift my chin. "I am sorry, my CV doesn't inspire you. It's true, I'm new to the fae realm. I assure you, fighting for what I believe in isn't new to me. The five of us will come together and make the fae realm proud in the days to come."

The woman's gaze slides over me and stops longingly on Hawk. "Human, arrogant, and uneducated, a trifecta of unattractive characteristics in a mate, Barron. No wonder you sought to break the bond."

Power surges inside me and my skin burns hot.

Brant lets off a menacing growl as he scans the seated bank of leaders. They're wide-eyed and staring with a mixture of awe and fear.

Hawk turns with genuine surprise glimmering in his steel-gray eyes to see my skin aglow. "It's fine, Spitfire. She's testing you. I didn't say or do anything to sever our bond, I swear it. Now, let's hear them out and go."

Kotah slides his hand into mine and my energy immediately starts to ease. "All is well, *Chigua*. Breathe. Not here."

*Jaxx*

*Frickety-frack.* I step in front of Hawk and pull Calli to

my side to face the council. It's plain that the Minister of the Fae Council has spent private time with Hawk and is stirring up trouble. Why the hell would she make that known in front of a newly transitioned phoenix who hasn't come to grips with her fiery side? It's either stupid or suicidal, and the minister is neither.

I clear my throat and smile at the baffled assembly staring at Calli. What? Are they surprised that threatening and insulting a phoenix makes her angry? "Please, we were invited here tonight under the guise of learnin' more about our role in the days to come. What can you tell us about Calli's resurrection and what it means to our lives?"

It's Dane, the Feline Prime who answers. The broad-shouldered male possesses the keen gaze of a hunter and a full mane of tawny hair. Though I've never met him in person, his leonine genes are obvious. "When your Pride Alpha contacted us to inform us of your account of Calliope's resurrection, I admit, we were skeptical."

I glance sideways at Calli, her skin alight in a golden glow of flames threatening to break loose. My breath catches at the magnificence of her. Every. Damn. Time. She steals my breath every time I look at her.

There's no heat coming off her, so for now, I don't need to worry about her clothes bursting into flame and clawing out the eyes of the Fae Council for gawking at my mate.

The leader of the goblin race is next to speak. "There is no doubt of her resurrection. I sensed the truth of her designation the moment the five of you stepped into the mezzanine at the great hall. As improbable as it is, here you all are."

"And now that your skepticism is satisfied," Hawk says, retaking his place to my left. He passes an impartial gaze across the panel of fae assessing us, seemingly unaffected by their nobility. "What have you to tell us about our next steps on this journey? Surely, within the recorded histories of eleven races, there must be a mention of a phoenix's calling."

Dane frowns. "I regret to say we don't know much. We can, however, give you something that is meant for one of you, and indirectly her."

An old man stands next to Dane in the arced line of leaders. He's a dryad judging by the wooden complexion and the branches protruding from his leafy nest of hair. He reaches a gnarled hand into the front of his robe and exposes the pith of his chest. The crack of wood splintering has all of us wincing.

The Goblin representative holds the dryad's shoulders steady as Dane bends and reaches into the trunk of the old man's chest. When he straightens, he holds a gemstone between his thumb and first finger.

He raises it and the crystal catches the light. "The Elder Council was entrusted with a piece of the guardian crystal. Four pieces combine to create the full phoenix's pendant. The legends state the pendant won't be whole until your committed bond as guardians and phoenix is whole."

"Where are the other pieces?" Hawk asks.

"We don't know."

"How do we find out?"

Dane shrugs. "Don't know that either."

*Frickety-frack.* Calli, Hawk, and the others look as

unimpressed as I'm sure I do. It's not encouraging when the most highly revered members of a magical world don't know shit about anything. Thanks for that.

Dane pins us with a look and continues. "The point of the next few days and weeks, and of reuniting the pieces of the pendant itself, is to reveal your innate abilities and hone them to the highest degree. You five need to align as mates and build your bond. Calliope needs to find her phoenix. There is a lot to do in a very short time."

The crystal rises from Dane's palm and floats in the air toward us. Hawk steps forward to pluck it from the ether, but it zaps him with a shock as he tries to touch it. He pulls back with a hiss, shaking his hand.

Brant snickers behind us. I fight not to laugh. The crystal floats closer, pauses in front of Kotah, and then Calli, and then hovers in front of me. When I raise my open palm, the crystal drops into my hand.

A surge of magical energy bombards my cells. My cat roars and my muscles tremble with an influx of strength. My knee hits the platform as I drop to absorb the onslaught. It's both terrifying and invigorating at the same time.

Golden rays burst out of me and radiate like a visible shockwave into the room. As the energy pulse hits and passes through the others, my bond with the quint locks into place.

The awareness of a vague presence in the back of my mind shifts and strengthens into something more—much more. They are a visceral part of me now. My pride. My pack.

They are *mine*.

*Hawk*

The five of us say nothing after the golden boy's power surge and light show. I thank the council members for their help, hit the switch to descend the platform, and wait until we're sealed into the antechamber before I unleash my curiosity. "What the hell was that, jaguar?"

Jaxx ass plants on the platform and blinks up at the ceiling looking dazed. Thank the Powers he had the vigilance to hold back his collapse until they were alone. Taking a dive in front of the elders wouldn't instill much confidence.

"Jaxx," Calli says, hiking the skirt of her dress so she can drop down beside him. "Are you okay?"

The guy's arm curls around her hips and he rolls them until he's lying over her and has his tongue down her throat. His cat lets off a throaty purr and we all groan as the flare of Calli's arousal blooms.

Brant adjusts his stance and chuckles. "So, that's a yes to the jaguar's health check as well as Calli's responsiveness. How about we take this show on the road?"

Kotah helps Calli to her feet and Jaxx gets up as if reassessing the world around him. He holds his open palm out and we all lean in to take a closer look at the crystal. Rounded over the top, it looks like a crystal pie wedge. Only, this wedge glistens and glows with what looks like a swirling eddy of water within.

"Miraculous," Kotah says. "Did you know three races of pixie harness the power to enchant crystals with elemental strengths?"

"Is that what you think this is?" Calli says, brushing

her finger over the stone. “It’s quite pretty.”

Kotah adjusts his glasses and looks closer. “Yes. If I were to guess, I’d say this crystal chose the guardian with the strongest elemental traits toward water and its characteristics.”

“Yeah?” Jaxx says. “How do you mean?”

“You proved yourself an accomplished swimmer when you rescued Calli from the pond. Your cat moves with aqueous strength and fluidity. And when confronted with an obstacle, you remain unhindered by conflict, divert, and stay the original course like a stream facing a rock in its path.”

I chuff. “That’s a philosophical stretch, kid. My money is on the gem picking him because he and Calli have already explored the mating mojo and gone the twenty toes route.”

It chaffs me raw that Jaxx claimed that ‘first’ as well.

Yes, part of my pique is alpha competitiveness but it’s also personal. Calli doesn’t care for my power or money or standing in life. Assessing me male-to-male against three others, she finds me wanting.

I’ll never admit it, but that hurts.

I reclaim my guns and sheath them ready to leave. “In any case, the enchanted gem chose you, jaguar, so put it somewhere safe.”

Calli steps off the platform and moves toward the door. “It sucks to assemble a puzzle and end up missing a piece.”

“Maybe you should hold onto it, hotshot,” Brant says, his chest bouncing as he pegs me with a cocky smile. "Go ahead, Hawk. Try to touch it again. I could use a good belly laugh."

They all get a kick out of that.

"Yuck it up, Bear. It's not the first time I've been rebuffed by the universe for being the first to try something. The point there is, I'm the first to try while others sit back and watch. I lead the pack."

The significance of that statement is lost on him. Whatever. I needn't explain myself or my strengths to the riffraff. I check my phone. Lukas has been busy in the last half-hour.

Good. Let us end a chapter in this mess, so we can move on to the next. I leave the others to gather their weapons and talk trash about me and join Calli.

With her arms crossed, the rounds of her breasts threaten to burst free of the bodice of the ice-blue gown. "What's the heated glare about, Spitfire?"

She pegs me with a ball-shriveling stare, and I regret asking. "Speaking of you leading the pack, Barron, I'd like to revisit the clusterfuck of that Minister clawing at me. How often have you bathed in her ambrosia?"

*Fuck.* I hoped that got lost in the shuffle. Guess not.

"Is this what I have to look forward to?" Her icy tone calls the attention of the others, but thankfully her ire seems to extend to Brant and Jaxx as well. "I've never been a jealous bitch but something inside me has changed. I get that you each had sex lives before me, but if your past conquests are going to insult me and throw it in my face that you planted your flag with them first, I won't handle it well."

I scratch my jaw. "Aleandi had no reason to disclose

our indiscretions. I don't know why she would. And I never reached out about severing our bond. That was a lie to get a rise out of you."

"Yeah, I picked up on that too," Jaxx says, curiosity in his tone. "What was the point of her little test?"

"Maybe to see how far I can ram my fist down her skinny, bendy-straw throat?" Calli snaps. "Because that's where I was headed until Kotah settled me."

Calli turns and offers Kotah a genuine smile. "Thank you for that, by the way. And thank you even more for keeping your cock in your pants. I am so grateful for your restraint."

Kotah blinks and then casts us an apologetic glance to us. "You're welcome?"

"Okay. New rule," Calli says, clapping her hands together. "If one of your sexual conquests comes into my orbit, I want a quick heads up, so I'm not blindsided."

The others look as wide-eyed horrified with the ex-lover arrangement as I am.

"That's a terrible idea," Jaxx says. "That will serve no purpose other than to upset you, kitten."

"It upset me to have a stranger making fuck-me eyes at one of my guardians and me feeling like a schmuck who arrived late to the party."

I open my mouth and hesitate. Since when do I bother to explain myself to anyone? I sigh… Since Calliope Tannis burst my life into flames, that's when. "Calli, consider the fact that you were raised human. By your admission, you've had a handful of partners in your entire life."

"What about it?"

"We're wildlings and are animals by nature. Sex doesn't mean the same thing to us. We grow up fucking in the form of humans or animals. It can be about anger or dominance or our animals letting off steam. Jaxx, Brant, and Kotah are pack members. Sexual connections increase the bonds of their community. Avians are different again because we're solitary animals and use sex to gain leverage and alliances."

She draws back, her gaze narrow. "So, of the hundreds of women you guys were with, you're saying none of them held any deep, personal meaning to you?"

"That's exactly what I'm saying."

She turns to the jaguar and I catch the flare of panic a split-second before I figure out why. "Is that how you feel, Jaxx? Will our morning together join the many non-personal wildling sexcapades you've participated in?"

"No," Jaxx says, and he gets full points for the ring of certainty. "This morning was transformative. I told you that and I meant it. You are in a different category altogether. Everything about you is personal to me."

"But you agree with Hawk otherwise? That the horizontal hijinks you all got into in the past is irrelevant. That it means nothing. That our lives began at the side of the road and everything that happened before that is forgotten."

Jaxx hesitates and I don't blame him.

That sounds like a lose-lose question.

"Calli," I say, stepping in to stop the carnage. "Perhaps we can table this domestic squabble for now and get out of here. The wolf needs to return home and we have one quick stop before we move on—something

I think you'll be more interested in than our past conquests."

Calli's eyes shift like liquid emeralds as she pegs me with a hostile gaze. "And what is that?"

"Sonny and the Sovereign Sons. I have a jet fueling on the tarmac if you still want to settle your score."

# CHAPTER NINETEEN

*Brant*

*Fucking asshole.* As the five of us climb into Hawk's sleek Gulfstream G650ER private jet, every instinct I have fires to life. The avian had no right to invite Calli into a confrontation with the leader of a drow gang. She isn't ready. Despite how naturally skilled she is, she's not ready for a head-to-head with males like that. And then there's this luxury lounge area with wings. Are we supposed to be impressed?

Okay, the way the others sink into the plush leather, captain's chairs and swivel, grinning at each other, it's obvious *they* are impressed, but they shouldn't be. Hawk has more money stacked in his coffers than a mint, but it's far less impressive when you consider the man.

"Is everything all right, Brant?" Kotah asks, leaning in from his seat. "You're unusually quiet."

"People don't plan murders out loud." I grab the seatbelt and sling it over my lap to buckle in.

The four of us settle into our seats, while Hawk goes up to speak with the pilot. Lukas stops on his way past us toward the area behind us with the plush three-seater sofas. "Your bags are in the aft stateroom. We have a few minutes if you want to change and freshen up. I'll show you where."

"Thank goodness," Calli says, jumping to her feet. "Me first. I gotta get out of this dress."

"I can help you with that, kitten," Jaxx says.

"Not this time, puss," she says, following Lukas's lead toward the back of the plane. "But I like the way you think."

Five minutes later, the four of us are changed and back to feeling more like ourselves. Jaxx found some pillows and blankets in one of the overhead storage bins and we are set for hunkering down for the flight.

Calli takes a deep breath as she sets herself up. "I wouldn't have survived growing up in a fancy world, I tell you that. I prefer breathing in my clothes."

Jaxx chuckles, buckles in and reaches over Calli's lap to ensure she's secure. The thunder of the engines builds, as the plane readies to get us moving.

"Speaking of growing up fancy," I say, turning to Kotah and switching gears for a moment. "I'm sorry about your dad, buddy. I don't know the guy, personally, but he's well respected as a strong leader and a male of honor. I'm sorry he's not doing well."

Kotah shrugs and purses his lips. "The Fae Prime may be a well-respected leader, but he is rubbish as a father. He has no interest in having a scholar for a son and made the shortfall of my intelligence known at every opportunity."

"That sucks." I've visited enough domestic scenes to know people don't understand what happens behind closed doors. "For what it's worth, the Prime failing to see how gifted you are is totally on him."

Calli nods and reaches across the space between us to take his hand. "It's his loss. You impress the hell out of us every day."

"Damn straight," Jaxx says, pushing back to recline. "You're here because the universe sees your worth. You rose above every other wolf in your line as the male to represent. That says a fuck ton more than a male blinded by arrogance."

Calli smiles and leans back, adjusting the blanket in her lap. "Exactly how much is a fuck ton?"

I chuckle. "I think it's fifty times a shit ton."

"Good to know."

That gets a smile out of the kid. I pat his wrist. "S'all good, buddy. You don't need to measure up to anyone. You have us now."

The jet starts a slow roll. Pushing back from its spot by the hanger, we start taxiing toward the runway. As much as I hate it, there's no way Calli will walk away from the opportunity to exact her revenge on the males who killed her friend.

Still, maybe we can mitigate the danger.

"Thinking ahead to the battle to come," I say, rubbing my palms together. "I need to voice my concern about putting you in harm's way, beautiful. You did well this afternoon in training, but these men—"

Calli frowns and leans forward in her seat. "Let me stop you now, Bear. There's no scenario where I don't avenge Riley. I understand that it's your first instinct to protect me, but my participation in this is not up for discussion."

"It's been a day," Kotah says, squeezing both armrests of his chair before pushing back to recline in his seat. "We have five hours until we reach California. Let's try to rest."

"Good idea," Jaxx says, crossing his arms over his chest and closing his eyes. "Lukas, can you dim the cabin interior?"

As the three of them close their eyes, I get the picture.

My concerns don't rank. Alrighty then. I cross my arms over my chest and shut my mouth. Why I am the only one of the four of us opposed to this, I have no idea.

This will come back and bite us in the ass. I feel it.

Fucking hell.

*Calli*

When we arrive at the remote property in Northern California, the five of us pile out of a blacked-out Navigator almost identical to Hawk's. It's four a.m. and the chill of the night works its way into the marrow of my bones. I shiver. Riley always said that an icy chill running up your spine means a ghost is near. Is she here with me? Does she know how much I miss her… how much I love her… that I'm going to make Sonny and his guys pay for hurting her?

Hawk escorts us to the back of the truck and opens things up. The storage space is filled with tactical gear, guns, and a dozen things I have no clue about.

He throws a vest over his head and secures the sides. "Lukas, you and Brant check in with the team and secure our approach. The two of you will join the lead strike and clear our path. Kotah, I want your wolf guarding Calli's back. You've got the strongest sense of smell and I don't want any surprises sneaking up on us. Jaxx, you and I are her bodyguards. She gets in, takes her moment and then she's outtie."

I frown at everyone deciding my life for me, but don't say anything. I have no frame of reference to argue and by the sounds of it, Hawk's trying to give me what I want the safest way possible.

Brant and Lukas each don on a Kevlar vest and head off. Kotah steps to the side door of the truck to shift and check out our surroundings. And Jaxx takes the moment to step into the shadows and empty his bladder.

Hawk pulls a vest over my head and gets me covered. "You're sure you want to do this?"

I pull my hair free from the back of the vest. "Positive."

He grabs a gun from a locked safe in the floor of the truck and presses it in my hand. "This gun has special ammunition that takes down drow. It negates any magical healing, but it doesn't stop them from retaliating with their powers. Be sure of your shot and shoot to kill. A head shot is tough for a new shooter. Aim for his chest, understood?"

I nod, a knot forming in my gut.

Hawk's gaze narrows and he checks over my shoulder. "Calli, listen to me. It's very different taking life in cold blood than it is fighting to save yourself or someone you love in the middle of a heated battle. Murdering Sonny will give him a place inside you that you'll never get back. I have no problem being the one who—"

"No," I say, swallowing my nerves. "It has to be me."

A flash of emotion flickers in his cold gray eyes.

"What?" I say after he falls silent.

"It takes one, to know one, remember?"

I shrug, not sure what he's getting at.

"I feel the shadow inside you. I know you're afraid to let the others see but if you kill Sonny right in front of them, it won't be your dirty little secret anymore. Are you sure snuffing out a piece of shit is worth it? Once people see the ruthless inside you, they look at you differently."

I pull oxygen into my lungs but it's an effort. He's right. While the others see me as a beacon of strength, Hawk sees the entire picture. There is a side of me I thought I kept hidden from all of them. It doesn't surprise me Hawk knows better.

"There are parts of me I'm not proud of, but for this quint bonding to work long term, I have to be authentic. If that tarnishes their image of me, they need to adjust and accept. I'm not sure how other wildlings handle mating bonds, but I won't lie about who I am. Like you said, 'As your past forged you into the male you are, my past forged me. I can be no other.'"

I can't tell if it's disappointment or respect clouding his gaze. "Does that make me less in your eyes?"

"Quite the opposite. You surprise me at every turn."

I search his expression. "You're a hard man to read. One minute you hate me. The next, you're organizing the five of us on our journey. The next, I'd swear I see a spark of hope in your eyes."

"First off, I never hated you. The situation, yes. My loss of control, definitely. I am, however, smart enough to separate you from what you represent. Second, I don't do hope. It's dark, you're tired, and your eyes are playing tricks on you."

*Yeah, no. I don't think so.* "So, you swear you didn't talk to the council about how to remove yourself from our quint."

"I told you that already." I'm sure he picks up on the erratic rhythm of my heart because he frowns and shakes his head. "That doesn't mean I'm staying."

"It means something."

He rolls his eyes. "It means that I didn't rise to the heights I have by making rash decisions. Being selected as a Guardian of the Phoenix is monumental. I haven't even begun to explore what that might mean to me moving forward."

His words blow a bazooka-sized hole through my hope.

Jaxx joins us, a screwed-up scowl marring face. "So, you're assessing your place in our quint as a future business opportunity for political advantage? Seriously, you're fucked up, Hawk."

I feel Hawk's defensive wall slam back into place.

"He's being honest. Everyone gets to voice their opinion even if you don't agree."

Jaxx turns his scowl on me. "So, you're okay with that? He gets a pass on sizing us up and deciding if it's worth his valuable time and money to answer the call of our people?"

"It's better than him blowing smoke up our asses

and lying. Yes, I'd much rather know where he stands."

Hawk checks his guns, replaces them into his shoulder holsters, and hits the button to close and lock the tailgate. "As much fun as it is to have you arguing about me when I'm standing right here, the bear is back. Yet another domestic dispute which will have to wait."

I leave a deeply disgruntled Jaxx and follow Hawk toward the mouth of the trail that leads to the Son's property. We haven't gone twenty feet before Kotah trots along at my hip. My fingers draw through the depths of his coat. Long, wiry guard hairs catch the light of the descending moon, making the velvety soft undercoat look black in the bleached light.

The relief of touching Kotah is immediate. I fill my lungs, my cells steadier simply by connecting with him.

Maybe Hawk's right and taking Sonny's life will change me in the eyes of Kotah, Jaxx, and Brant. Everything is still so new with them. We're all testing the waters of our new normal, putting our best foot forward. We all want this to work out. Even Hawk… I think.

My avian mate turns to me at the edge of a clearing. A sprawling ranch bungalow sits in darkness, sleeping in the early hours before dawn. "You have your gun?"

I lift it to show him, careful to keep it pointed out at the clearing. "Point and squeeze, right?"

He reaches over and releases a catch with his thumb. "That's right. If at any time you want me to take the shot, let me know. I don't want you carrying the weight of this unless you're one-hundred percent sure."

"Listen to him," Brant says, pushing into our

conversation. "Your friend is dead, and nothing will make that better. She will be avenged, and these assholes won't hurt any other women. You don't have to pull the trigger."

My temper flares and my hair blows back from my face as a wild chinook suddenly engulfs us. "It *does* have to be me. Imagine someone tortures, rapes, and mutilates Doc. They leave the body on your doorstep, so you find him. Do you pass the buck and let someone else take care of it or do you make it right?"

The answer glows in his golden eyes. He doesn't like it, but he's starting to get the picture.

"Take me off the pedestal, Bear. I never agreed to be your paragon of inspiration and don't want the job. This is me. Like it or not. Stop painting me with a delicate brush."

I hate the flare of emotion in his warm golden eyes, but it's said, and I won't take it back. He stomps off, the bass rumble of his bear's growl rattling in my chest.

I turn to Hawk once he's gone and nod. "Okay enough overanalyzing. Let's get this party started."

He taps the comm system he has in his ear. "Move in. Secure the building. It's a go."

*Kotah*

Hawk's team navigates the darkness like lethal shadows consuming everything in their path. Brant is among them and it both impresses me that he does this for a living and unnerves me how much the danger of him being in a front-line offensive worries me. He's more than one of Calli's other mates… he's fast becoming another of my mates.

I file that realization away for the moment and focus on the situation at hand. The first team disarms the perimeter security, infiltrates the house, and after a pregnant pause of silence, reports in.

Hawk responds to something he hears through his earpiece and nods. "Well done. Allow the bear to secure the situation to his satisfaction. When he's confident the phoenix is safe, we'll move in."

Calli blinks up at him, a growing affection warming her gaze. "Careful, Hawk. That almost seemed thoughtful. You wouldn't want us to get the wrong impression."

Hawk chuffs. "Whatever else the bear might be—pain in the ass, hot-head, self-righteous furball—I reviewed his files. He's an outstanding FCO enforcer and he's worried about you. If he secures that house to his liking, you'll be safe, and we can all—" he taps his ear and nods. "Understood. The phoenix is landing. We're coming in."

*Calli*

Despite the buildup and Hawk's pep talks, seeing Sonny cable-tied to a chair in the kitchen of the house stirs nothing inside me except conviction. Maybe I'm numb to the idea of morality or maybe it simply doesn't apply to him given what he put Riley through, but for all Hawk's concern about me suffering about taking a life, I don't.

I step right up to where the mouthy, blond, master of nothing sits glaring at me, raise the gun Hawk gave me, and pull the trigger. *Bang.*

Hawk's wrong about another thing too. The head shot isn't hard. As the gun fires and the scent of weapon discharge tingles in my sinuses, I watch the spray of blood and brain matter explode against the wall behind Sonny.

And I'm glad.

His head slumps forward and I let off another couple of rounds into his chest. Unlike the shock and disbelief that overcame me when I fried Plaid Nightmare, this kill brings out another kind of emotion.

Satisfaction.

Just so everyone is clear on that, I meet the gaze of each of my guardians. "This is me, boys. Sorry, if that doesn't sit well, but there you have it. He hurt someone I love, and I won't apologize for wanting him dead. I'd do the same for any of you."

And with that, I hand Hawk my gun, and leave the whole mess behind me.

An hour later, I exit the lavatory at the back of Hawk's private jet and frown at the empty aft stateroom. Both couches are lowered and berthed out to provide a wall-to-wall bed, the pocket door is closed, and the lights are dimmed. It's spacious and welcoming and heart-breakingly empty. I flop down on the cushioned surface and pull the soft micro-fiber blanket over myself.

Reality check. My guardians saw behind the veil of who I am and obviously, they didn't like the view.

I brush my fingers over the console behind my head and abandon the idea of asking one of them to join me. If

I ask, they don't really want to be here. No way do I want any of them running through the motions.

That's the whole point.

I roll onto my stomach and look out the portal window to watch the lights of San Francisco twinkling far below. The city looks so beautiful from a distance. But like anything, if you get too close, you see the flaws.

That's how things work, right?

With my lungs compressing in my chest, I force myself to breathe and backtrack to the intercom button. Pressing down, the button lights up under my finger.

"As a kid, I used to look up to planes flying overhead and wonder about the lives of the people on board. Were they rich? Were they happy? Were they going somewhere exotic? Were they as lonely as I was? My parents were dead. My aunt and uncle betrayed me. I was living on the streets and had nothing… I had no one."

My eyes burn as I focus on the land below and blazing golden light pops up over the line of the horizon. "When Riley found me, I'd been on my own for three months, I hadn't eaten in days, I'd been shaken down for my shoes, and I was terrified that if I went to a shelter or a soup kitchen they'd send me back to my uncle."

I picture Riley that day, sweeping my hair back and saying. *'You look like shit, girlfriend. You better come with me.'*

"She said she lived in a palace and to us, that's what it was. She had a fort made of old boxes and broken skids propped behind a Chinese food restaurant. When I got there, she went straight to work building an addition so I could have my own wing. The rest is history. We were a team."

I close my eyes against the sunrise and flop onto my back. "When I found her lying face down in a puddle in the alley beside our apartment, the light in my life snuffed out. We had so many hopes. We saved up for three years to get that shitty one bedroom, but we didn't care. It had a toilet and a lock on the door, and we were safe from the dangers of the streets. We could build a new life. I bought into the illusion… then, she was taken away too."

I stare up at the ceiling of the plane and draw in a labored breath. It feels like a tank is sitting on my chest, keeping my lungs from filling with air. "I told Jaxx that first day that I've never made it work with any guy… but over the past four days, I decided to try. I'm learning on the fly here, and I'm sorry if I'm not who you want me to be, but I won't pretend to be someone I'm not."

I swipe at the tears warming my cheek and marvel at how far I've come in a week. "Anyway, that's all I had to say. We can talk about it when we get to Kotah's community… or not. I'll let you decide because I honestly don't know what the hell I'm doing, so… yeah, that's it. Over and out."

The button ceases glowing green when I press it with my thumb, and I pull the shade to block the window. The last thing I need is to see the shiny happy promise of a new day when my life is stuck in sucksville.

"Calli? May I come in, *Chigua?*"

"Only if you want to. I don't want a pity party."

The pocket door glides across its track. Kotah ducks inside and climbs onto the eight-foot by eight-foot bed.

He crawls on his hands and knees until he's beside me and flops down. "I would've been here all along, but the others thought you needed a moment to yourself to grieve your friend."

"By myself?" My tears fall in earnest and I curl against his chest. "I hate being by myself. I thought you guys were pulling away from me."

"Aw, kitten," Jaxx says, climbing aboard. He lays on my other side and pulls me into a full-body hug. "Never gonna happen. We're a lock, remember? Four males dedicated to meeting your needs, ensuring your safety, and devoted to helping you in the trials to come. Any of this sound familiar?"

Brant crawls in and stops Kotah from moving away. "No, buddy, she needs your comfort. You soothe our girl."

He lays perpendicular to the three of us at the end of the bed and squeezes my feet. When he looks up at me, I'm engulfed by the emotion in his gaze. "We won't always see eye-to-eye, beautiful, but that's worlds away from not wanting you or what this bonding represents. You were right. If someone did that to my family, I'd snap their neck. Eye for an eye. Life for a life. It was misogynistic to expect different from you simply because you're our female. Forgive me."

I draw a deep breath and take a page out of Jaxx's book. "Forgiven. Forgotten."

The four of us settle into our love in and I can't help but watch the empty doorway. Come on, Hawk. Be one of us. Except, he doesn't come. I close my eyes and reach out along the mating bond to find him outside the door.

He's close. He's angry. And fighting the mating bond.

"I'm hoping for an appearance, Mr. Barron, not a commitment. And hey, the last show of mating faith worked out all right. My lips are still stinging from that kiss. I'm breathless anticipating where we go from there."

Hawk fills the doorway and rolls his eyes. "Like I said before, Spitfire. You couldn't handle it."

"And like I said, *Challenge accepted.*"

## ***~~ End Note ~~***

Thank you for reading Rise of the Phoenix. I hope you enjoyed getting to know Calli and her guardians in their first days together. Things start heating up fast in book two and we get a deeper understanding of who these five are and how they're going to fit together…(pun intended).

If you are inclined to help a girl out, it would be amazing if you could leave a star rating or review on Amazon.

If you want more, click here and snag your copy of book two, Wolf's Soul

***Author Notes: May 1, 2020***

After writing 18 fantasy, paranormal, and sci-fi sexy/steamy monogamous romance novels, it was time to get my sexy on and expand into the realm of polyamory.

Why choose, right?

Guardians of the Phoenix was originally planned as a 4-book series, but after huge popularity, has been expanded to a fifth book. It is the first Reverse Harem series I've written and I've gotta say, it's fun to have more sexy times to spread around. I hope these guys give you hours of entertainment and escape.

JL

**Find Me**


Amazon, Facebook, Twitter, Instagram

Web page – www.jlmadore.com

Email – jlmadorewrites@gmail.com


**Guardians of the Phoenix (Shifter Reverse Harem)**

Book 1 – Rise of the Phoenix

Book 2 – Wolf's Soul

Book 3 – Bear's Strength

Book 4 – Hawk's Heart

Book 5 – Jaguar's Passion

**The Watchers of the Gray Series (Paranormal)**

Book 1 – Watcher Untethered (Zander)

Book 2 – Watcher Redeemed (Kyrian)

Book 3 – Watcher Reborn (Danel)

Book 4 – Watcher Divided (Phoenix)

Book 5 – Watcher United (Seth)

Book 6 – Watcher Compelled (Bo)

Book 7 – Watcher Unfeigned (Brennus)

Book 8 – Watcher Exposed (Hark)

**The Scourge Survivor Series (Fantasy)**

Book 1 – Blaze Ignites

Book 2 – Ursa Unearthed

Book 3 – Torrent of Tears

Book 4 – Blind Spirit

Book 5 – Fate's Journey

Book 6 – Savage Love

**Aliens of Atlantis Series (Sci-Fi)**

Book 1 – Taryn's Tiderider

Book 2 – Kai's Captive

Book 3 – Alyandra's Shadow

**In the Shadow of Vesuvius (Roman Time-Slip)**

In The Shadow of Vesuvius

**Auburn Tempest**

**Pen Name for Fantasy Action Adventure (Not Romance)**

**Misty's Magick and Mayhem Series**

Book 1 – School for Reluctant Witches

Book 2 – School for Saucy Sorceresses

Book 3 – School for Unwitting Wiccans

Book 4 – Nine St. Gillian Street

Book 5 – The Ghost of Pirate's Alley

Book 6 – Jinxing Jackson Square

Book 7 – Flame

Book 8 – Frost

**Exemplar Hall**

Prequel – Death of a Magi Knight

Book 1 – Drafted by the Magi

Book 2 – Jesse and the Magi Vault

Book 3 – The Makings of a Magi

Made in the USA
Columbia, SC
07 October 2020